W9-CNW-117

THE THINGS WE DO TO

MAKE IT HOME

New York *Random House*

BEVERLY GOLOGORSKY

THE THINGS

WE DO

TO MAKE IT

HOME

A Novel

Copyright © 1999 by Beverly Gologorsky

All rights reserved under International and Pan-American
Copyright Conventions. Published in the United States by
Random House, Inc., New York, and simultaneously in
Canada by Random House of Canada Limited, Toronto.

Library of Congress Cataloging-in-Publication Data
Gologorsky, Beverly.
The things we do to make it home : a novel / Beverly Gologorsky.
1st ed.
p.   cm.
ISBN 0-375-50201-7
1. Vietnamese Conflict, 1961–1975—Veterans—United
States—Fiction.   I. Title.
PS3557.0447T47   1999   813'.54—dc21   98-21099

Random House website address: www.randomhouse.com
Printed in the United States of America on acid-free paper
9 8 7 6 5 4 3 2
First Edition

Book design by J. K. Lambert

FOR

Charles Wiggins, my partner,

Georgina, my daughter,

AND

Tom Engelhardt, with deep appreciation

CAST OF CHARACTERS

Hundreds of thousands of women met, lived with, lost, and/or married the men who fought in Vietnam. Their names have never been collected, filed, or written down anywhere.

They include:

- Emma Hanson, who married Rod Devins
- Millie Reid, who married Leonard (aka Rooster) Barodin
- Lucy Reid (sister of Millie), who married Nick Santino
- Tess Evans, who married Sean (aka Sandwich) Metcalf
- Deede Cassidy, who married Jason Connors
- Ida Connors (sister of Jason), who loved Frankie Bower
- Pauli Bower (sister of Frankie)

CONTENTS

PART ONE

1973

We were in bed
We were sauced
We were plastered
We were stoned
We were drumming floors
We were bathed in TV light
We were alive
We were together
We were back in the world.

■ And she's still not used to the noises he makes in other rooms. She hears him pacing the floor and snapping his fingers as if he can't contain the ideas popping into his head.

Dropping the green cotton skirt over her silky green blouse, she thinks it's crazy, dressing up this way to watch TV, but

Rooster will twirl her around, three times at least, like she was the main show and he won't let it end. Before him, men were so ordinary, so predictable. He surprises her breath away, driving them into Manhattan at 3:00 A.M., the tall glass buildings filled with blue light and no people, his arm wrapping her waist. He never lets her stray from his side. Back home, they sneak upstairs, not waking her sister or Nick, hiding in bed till noon, their bodies tight together. It worries her the way he can go on with no sleep, expecting her to do the same, although when she can't he leaves her be, takes off by himself. Once they're married he'll settle down. He's just excited, the way she is, about everything.

Yesterday she missed her morning classes and arrived in a daze at the afternoon workshops, where the teacher was shagging hair. In the evening she found the time to perm the wig on her mannequin, which used to reside on the kitchen table until Rooster covered it and moved it to the window ledge. The eye sockets gave him the creeps. Soon she'll graduate and look for a full-time job. Rooster too. Then they can rent a place, their own, maybe buy it someday, and he can listen to music all night if he wants to.

She weaves the last strands of her hair into a French braid, and with arms faintly aching, slips the end into a barrette. Listen up, men, he'll say, Millie and I are getting married. She opens the closet door, studies the shoe rack. They agree, today is perfect for the announcement. They'll all be together. He'd better remember. She searches out her beige, high-heeled pumps.

■ He counts twenty-two steps from the bedroom door to the end of the living room. If he walks across the couch, it's only nineteen. He glances out the window. Looks like an afternoon storm that could last minutes, or days. No use trying to keep dry. The heavens are tricky. The key is not to care.

He switches on a lamp in the rapidly darkening room. Listens for the drumbeat of Millie's heels. She doesn't like him barging in while she's dressing. She says that he's got to give her some privacy. Soon there'll be thunder, lightning. He begins snapping his fingers. Twenty-two steps. He turns, fixes his eyes on the door. Twenty-two steps. Hey, baby, anchors need to be close to their boats.

He switches on another lamp, drops into a chair. A thunderclap rumbles deep in his chest. This vessel's ready to steer out of here. He stands up. Twenty-two steps. He looks for a magazine. None in sight.

He glances out at the yellow house across the street. A patch of grass black as the sky.

He flicks on the TV. Nothing. Goddamn box. Not even plugged in. Jesus. He can't be prowling around looking for a socket. Shit. Twenty-two steps. He opens the bedroom door. "Hey, baby."

She's slipping on her shoes. He wraps his arms around her, nuzzles his face into her clean-smelling hair. Make love, he thinks, so deep inside he'll hear nothing but the feathery sounds that come off her breath.

"Don't mess me."

He unzips her skirt. "You can't be messed, baby."

"They'll be here soon."

"They'll be late. They're always late." He sits her on his lap. "Pretty bird, why should we ever leave this room?" He slips off the barrette, begins unbraiding her silky, orange-red hair that's like a morning sun, a 'Nam moon. He traces the line of freckles marching down her neck. "We need to count these." He peers into her green saucer eyes scattered with infinite black and yellow specks. "Tiger eyes."

"Ever see one?"

"Heh, heh. They saw me." He lifts her blouse over her head.

"Don't undress me anymore." She shakes her shoulders.

"Why not?" He lays her on the bed, sliding up beside her.

"Don't you want to go the party, Rooster?"

His name, that name, still so strange from her lips. "We will. I'll dress you."

"Let's not be late. They'll all be there, except Lucy and Nick."

Filled with the after-sweet tiredness of loving her, he might be able to sit still for the car ride. "Right. Can't expect him to leave the bubble till the bluebird flies through Manhattan."

"He's home as long as you are."

"Maybe yes, maybe no."

"Riddles again."

"But you understand them."

"Do I?"

"I'm the middle of the riddle and you're marrying me anyway."

"Be serious."

"Serious is a hole in the hourglass." Her pale brows create little frown lines like a puppy's, low on her forehead. He needs to take her with him into oblivion. He rubs the back of his hand on her soft cheek. "I'd rather do carefree."

"You need to do something."

"Yeah, something."

"Like school. The government will pay."

"They can't pay me what they owe me, sweet bird."

"Let it go, Rooster. It's over for you. Forget it."

"Forgotten, baby, like old garbage. It just stinks, that's all. Hey, I've got it figured: you're a beautician, so I'll be a barber. We'll open a shop, serve bubbly while we cut, and charge the men extra for seeing you. Except no grunts." His fingers play along her arm.

"How come?"

"They need the hair. To cover their mugs, the shaggy bastards."

She lifts his beard. "Nothing hidden there."

"You smell so good." He presses himself against her softness. One hand finds the knob of her hipbone, holding on not to glide away. "Whatever you want," he whispers, not sure why.

"Do you mean it?"

"You name it," he whispers again.

"I want a house someday."

"One place for the rest of your life?" He lifts the round breast out of the bra cup.

"Why not?"

"What about camping out?"

"Once in a while."

"With just sleeping bags."

"Okay."

"Good. Because I saw this large estate in South Hampton. We could set up a hooch facing the water, cook on the beach. No one's there after October."

"But we'll be working then."

"It's our shop. We're the bosses. We can take our vacations when we want." He slides back up and looks into round, flecked eyes full of doubt. "Smile, Millie. What's the worst thing that could happen?" His lips on hers, searching for the immediate warmth.

▪ "Jason, Jason," he chides himself. "Caught short, man, short." He spreads the green, heart-shaped dexies on the kitchen table. Chips on a bingo card, except they cover only four spaces and he has twenty-four hours to get through before he can reach Seymour Pervert, SP to his friends. Damn. Damn. Contact's got to be made before tomorrow. He can't interview for anything on nothing. Won't be easy. Man doesn't live normally, has no phone, doesn't take checks. Pray he gets his message at the rug store and arrives with a pocketful in the morning. He'll borrow some cash from his sister. Ida's shy on asking questions. Not Deede, though. A hint'll get you a million from her. He'll head for Manhattan before dawn, before she wakes, leave a note saying he went to Jones Beach. Not much of a lie. They should never have downpaid on this place. No one scores an easy hit in the burbs. Except Deede hates the city.

Whatever will he do later? Not even one downer. Shit! He'll be wearing eyeballs all night. He'll never kick the habit of staying alert in the dark.

Thank the good Buddha for Rod's party. Watergate Party. Beer, liquor too, that's for sure. Rod knows what the men need. If he tips enough sauce, that'll wipe out hours, and Frankie's driving both ways. Once they took care of each other. Now they're in separate holes. Fear opened them up. All those nights he talked away, confessing whatever lay on his chest. Like him rummaging that dead boy's body, still warm. What did he expect to find? A worthless photo that he'll never show to Deede. It might scare her, maybe away from him. Then where would home be?

He slides two pills into his palm. Studies them. He'll do these, then at two the next, and at five the final one. That should take care of the light time. He has to think strategically. No, that's the LT's job. His is to get through.

He takes the OJ out of the fridge, swallows the pills, and drinks until the pulpy, acidic taste clogs his throat. Shit! He pours the rest down the drain. Deede's letting the place rot. He glances at floor, walls, window. Immaculate. The way he likes it. No, she's okay. Her footsteps overhead. He wads the remaining two pills into a Kleenex and slips it in his pants pocket. He can't stay here, waiting to lift off. He advances on the stairs. "Deede? Deede!"

"What?"

He catches the urgency in his voice, sits down on a step. His eyes sweep the orderly living room. Calm, man, be calm. Not a mansion, but nifty. Fixed up just the way he wants. No greens. No earth colors at all. Sky, sun, and water, he told her, he can live with that. Yeah, he's starting to feel it. Only a little rush, but it's there. He stands. "I'm coming to get you."

She's there at the top in her little-boy pajamas. "Hey, we're going to be late," he says. "You want to keep Frankie's motor running?"

She slips her arms around his neck. "I want to talk about the party."

"Not again, come on."

"You're going to booze away the hours."

"We're going to sit in Rod's new house and watch Nixon's ass get whipped by the little pricks who worked for him."

She pushes past him. "I need a cup of coffee."

Light as a feather, strong as a horse. He follows her small, lithe body into the kitchen. She fills the kettle, flips on the gas. Quick, sharp movements. He glimpses her smooth olive cheeks, full pink lips. The girl doesn't need an ounce of makeup. "I'll have one, too, thick."

"It's too early for espresso."

"Not for me."

She checks out the dewy shine in his eyes, the red patches on his cheeks, then pulls the espresso machine off the shelf. Everyone gets stoned nowadays, she reminds herself. At least his hair isn't down to his ankles or crawling all over his face like the others.

"Let me help." He comes up behind her.

If they make love, he might consider forgetting the damn party. They can watch those clowns on their own TV. Actually, they don't have to leave the house at all. She relaxes against him.

"Want to skip the coffee?" She gyrates her hips. "Just phone them."

"And say what?" He drops the question into her hair.

"I don't know. That we were out late, can't make it." She slides her arm around his waist.

"They'll be disappointed." Still whispering.

"Tell them we'll get together soon. Let's go to bed, just for a while. You know we haven't loved for a few days." She beams at him.

Maybe a quickie. Shit. Not after the dexies. Shit. It'll take a lifetime to coax him hard now. Besides, he needs the men today.

"It's already set up, sweetheart. We have to be there." He kisses her cheek, then carefully moves away.

With one hand balled into a fist, she counts out spoonfuls of coffee. Why does she bother? He's on his way, that's for sure. The party will finish him, damn them all. "Play and noise. A whole day of it. I can't take it that long."

"Then have a few drinks. That's what parties are for."

"I don't like whiskey." She sits across from him at the table, staring.

"Smoke some dope. Lift off, just for an hour. Look down on the everyday shit." He reaches for her hand, turns it palm up. "See that life-line, that's money in the bank. The question is: how are you going to spend it?"

"We have zero in the bank."

"We're talking life-lines here."

The kettle screams.

He jumps up, knocking the chair. Catches it just in time. "Shut that fuckin' thing off."

She darts to the stove, kills the flame, pours the boiling water into the espresso pot.

"I'm sorry." His face flushed, his mouth a thin, tight line.

"*I'm* sorry." She says it in a voice meant to keep him calm. "Soon as it cools, the kettle's gone," she croons. "I'll turn on some music. We'll get in a party mood, okay? We're going to Rod's, aren't we?" She reaches out for him.

"Yeah, right," he mumbles, stepping back. "Sure as shit."

She straightens the chair.

"Go on, hurry, get dressed." She nods, watching him, then runs up the stairs. When she's out of sight, he grabs the bottle of scotch from the cabinet. There's only an inch left. He meant to save it for tonight. He tips the bottle to his mouth. The liquid burns a path down his throat. He pours espresso into a mug, pulls out the tissue, pops the remaining pills, drinks them down with sips of too-hot coffee. The kettle ruined his high. He needs to start again.

▪ Goddamn Chevy in front is crawling, and the road's too narrow to pass. Maybe he'll let Ida take the wheel. She's not a fan of his driving anyway. Probably he won't, probably he'll keep her near him so he can smell her sweetness, see her soft roundness under her light summer dress. He's the one with the edges. Right, Papa-san? He won't mention the truck to her, not yet. Independent movers rake in shitloads of money. The lifting, carrying, that'll be easy. Getting caught in traffic jams, that might bring on the Furies though. He returned with more cash than he's ever had. Now he has zilch, plus a truck.

The first cross-country trip, he'll take Ida. They'll sleep in motels, cheap, cozy, clean, with pictures on the walls that have no meaning, and neighbors who have no names. She'll like that.

With her brother out of the house, the place is finally hers; and he knows what's coming, it's natural, healthy, everyone's next step. But he can't marry, can't even move in. The sweet, loving nights spent with her, and he's awake until dawn, then guns the car onto the expressway, windows rolled down, doors unlocked, speeding past all possibility of surprise.

The car in front is taking its Sunday-school time. He presses the horn and doesn't let up either. At least he's out of the old drunk's place now. What a pair they make. Him waking up screaming from a nightmare, his father running in to ask who he is. Depressing. When Pauli was there, they ignored the old man, or tried to. He glances at the look-alike houses creeping by. Somehow, wherever his sister is, he knows she wouldn't live around here.

The last time he saw Pauli, that night before he left, a bad scene. She, trying to talk him out of it. His father yelling, "Frankie will do like other boys." She, stubborn. "I don't want some shiny-faced soldier handing me a flag. *We* can help you." Which was all his father needed. "*We* can help you? Who do you think you are, Ladybird!" She, pronouncing each word as if it were a warning. "You don't have to go. We have ways."

"Jail?" She, laughing. "I counsel men like him all week, strangers who will live, and not in jail either." Her hand trying to find his.

"Your coward friends will become doctors and he'll be an ex-con for the rest of his life."

"He doesn't have to be like you, a little man afraid of everything!"

The old drunk flinging her past the couch. She, lifting herself to her feet, and leaving with one last pleading look back at him but not a word.

Them, fighting over him like two dogs over raw meat.

He, following the arrows to the Jersey buses, hoping she'd turn up to say good-bye, walking down a dimly lit staircase, through a door, into the gray dawn.

Jesus, it was cold. He still remembers the little dance he was tapping out to keep warm when the door opened. Not Pauli, but a husky kid with wild yellow curls around a big, baby face.

"Fort Dix?" the kid asks.

"Yeah."

"Bus must be late, not that I care. If it never comes, can't go. Simple logic. The way I see it. We're theirs. No money, no kids. They know who to take. I mean, this could be the beginning of the end of our lives. So what's the rush? Simple logic. The way I see it, it's not Germany or Italy. It's tiger and monkey land."

The bus like the rush of Rod's words crashing down the ramp just to get them. And anything slower still makes him crazy.

He wonders if Rod even remembers that ride. He pokes his head out the window. The empty road is there somewhere. He may have to flatten a few lawns to get to it, but once he does, he can pedal the gas, lift the pressure off his head. Anyway, he can't be dawdling, Papa-san, Ida's waiting, his buddies, too. The good people, not the fools, liars, and jerk-offs.

He's riding the Chevy's bumper at minus ten miles an hour when suddenly it stops. His foot smashes the brake. A dog loping across the road. Jesus. Tremors play chords in his legs. "Still, man, be still," he mutters. Hey, Papa-san, what do I do? The Chevy creeps forward again, shining a spiteful chrome smile back at him. He strains to catch the image that pops into his head, but it's gone before he can grasp it, leaving only the terror, and the question—where will he be when it shows up again. The tremors are in his arms now, his body no longer listening to reason. He pulls the car over, jumps out, begins humping toward Ida's place. Pay attention, Papa-san, remember where we parked.

■ Emma does a slow turn in the middle of the living room. New beige carpet, new blue couch, new coffee table, new chairs, new nineteen-inch TV inside its sleek black console. And it scares her—all of it—because nothing has prepared her for luck. Not even Rod coming home intact. It's the whole cake, plus a well-stocked freezer. She's never owned a thing but her clothing. Now, an upstairs, a downstairs, even a basement that Rod's father plans to finish. And she believes him, too. He's a builder by nature as well as by trade, like Rod. And easy to keep books for. She makes no mistakes. Yesterday, when she pointed out an error on an invoice, it was as if she'd given him a gold brick, not a few extra dollars.

"Emma? Where is anything?" Rod stands at the head of the stairs, naked, a towel around his neck. "I had a system with all the boxes."

"In closets."

"My fatigues don't like closets."

"What exactly are you looking for?"

"Maybe a T-shirt?"

"In the chest of drawers, top one's yours."

"We're not sharing our drawers?" He flips off the towel, slides it around his waist. "Come here, do the dance."

She shakes her head and turns away. If only she could post a big, black-lettered sign:

SPILL A DRINK AND DIE!

FILTHY SHOES OFF THE COUCH!

NO JUMPING ON FURNITURE.

OR ELSE!!!

But they won't listen to orders or follow instructions. She'll have to watch Ida's brother carefully, Jason can get out of control, Rooster, too. Frankie worries her the least. She gazes at the maple tree, *their* maple tree, hers, which will turn red and yellow in the fall, so they say. It's beautiful to stand here when it gets dark outside and the house is lit around her.

While Rod was away she never chain-locked the apartment door. In case he arrived while she slept. The silliness of it often struck her, but she didn't dare change lest the gods take it out on him. She still leaves a night lamp burning to appease them. She's too happy. Anything could happen.

Her eyes slide down the quiet street. Their raucous coming will leave its imprint.

"What're you doing?" He steps up behind her, and tugs her toward the chair.

"Worrying that the men will forget this is our house and lay waste."

"Not funny."

She straddles his lap, facing him. "It's nice of us to have everyone visit. I mean, we spent a pretty penny for the food and I don't even know what you paid for the booze."

"Doesn't matter. They've earned the best, and I aim to please. Give a kiss."

She brushes his forehead with her lips. His face is amazingly round. His blond hair unbelievable. The only blond in his family. "Where'd you come from," she whispers.

"Listen, no tours of the house, okay?"

"Why?"

"Makes me uncomfortable."

"But they've never seen it before."

"Yeah, well, it's just a house. Wait until they get their own."

"Then turn on the hearings now. That way, they'll all sit down like at the movies." The beeping horn sends her off his lap. "Shut them up!" She pushes him toward the door. She doesn't even know the neighbors yet. In the vestibule, she hears Rod shouting, "This way, men!"

"A palace, son," Rooster says, peering over his granny glasses. "My man here's a sultan and I see the grapes." He nudges Frankie toward the bar that Rod's set up on the coffee table.

Ida kisses her cheek, squeezes her hand, whispers "Looks nice."

Ida's brother clicks the TV on. "Where are the little shits?" Jason begins switching from channel to channel.

"Wait a long minute." Rooster drops onto the floor near Millie. "Give the boys time for nature's calling."

Jason reaches for the scotch bottle.

She moves to lower the volume.

"Hey, Emma, no can make out." Jason turns it up again.

Deede places a restraining hand on his arm.

"Not now, sweetheart."

"Find Jason the hearings," Deede says.

"Man can discover such things for himself," Rooster mutters.

"Emma, how big are these digs?" Frankie asks.

"Three bedrooms upstairs, plus what you see down here."

Rooster whistles.

"This is the place for all good men to come to the aid of their friends," Rod recites.

"Who needs another scotch?" Jason holds up his already empty glass.

"Not you," Deede mutters.

"Man must do what he must do." Rooster passes Jason a new glass.

"What I do, I do well." Jason pours a heavy couple of inches into Rooster's glass and his own.

"Ought to hire yourself out as a bartender."

"He'll do better than that," Deede says. "He has an interview at a bank tomorrow."

"No shit." Frankie toasts him. "Doing what?"

"It's for a training program," Deede replies.

"My brother's very versatile," Ida tells them.

"Jason's been the banker for every crapshoot I won." Frankie drops a short laugh. "He needs no training."

"It doesn't translate into civilian life," Rod says seriously.

"Nothing does, my man."

"We're talking jobs," Deede snaps, "maybe even becoming a manager."

"You're talking jobs, sweetheart. Me, I'm having an interview. Hey, what's this?" Jason turns the volume up another notch.

"*General Hospital,*" Millie says. "It's depressing. Turn it off."

"Can't. Have to locate Nixon's men." Jason places his glass on top of the set and once again switches channels, stopping nowhere.

"Man's in an inquiring mood," Rooster quips.

"Someone *please* find Jason the hearings." Emma's voice echoes in her head, ratcheted up louder than the TV, way too loud. Rod throws her a disapproving glance, like she's the crazy one. Maybe she is, maybe she's gotten herself a role in a fantasy she never auditioned for. She kneels in front of the set. If she can find the hearings, perhaps it'll calm them down.

"Wait, don't make them disappear." Jason's at her side.

"It's just some soap opera," she whispers.

"Yeah, but that's the channel we want." Stubborn as a child. "Nixon's men are on their way." He sits back and stares into the screen.

"Why in hell would you want to see a bunch of ugly men when we have such lovely ladies right here?" Frankie nods in Ida's direction.

"We're a sight better than Nixon's flunkies." Millie tosses back her head. "Besides, why spend good time on bad people?"

"Especially when you have zilch in common with them," Deede mutters.

"The difference is here." Rod pats his butt. "They've got fat wallets."

"They're going to be out on the streets real soon," Ida says. "But, hey, who cares?"

"Even so," Rod continues, "nobody's going to pick their pockets. They'll never have to worry about money."

"Correct," Deede snaps. "Unlike you guys."

"These men can hold their own with the best of them." Millie kisses Rooster's cheek.

"The woman speaks the truth."

"Go ahead, put down what you can't have," Deede says.

"What's that?" Ida asks.

"Money, honey, no doubt there." Rod refills Frankie's drink.

"And trouble. Nixon's men got trouble, now," Rooster adds.

"Who gives a shit." Jason shrugs.

"True, fella, those men have not earned our concern. So turn off the glare, my man."

"Rooster," Millie chides, "we're not watching the hearings yet."

"I bet I can find those shits on *my* TV, something's wrong with yours."

"Drunk already." Deede shakes her head.

"We are the way we are," Jason tells her.

"High but mighty." Rooster flaps one arm.

"Down and out," Deede mumbles.

"That reminds me . . . where's Sean?" Frankie asks.

Deede shrugs. "Closeted with Tess is my guess."

"Incapacitated," Jason adds.

"Wrong word, right thought." Rooster grins.

"Deede gave him Tess, and they are busy, busy," Jason says.

"Busy?" Emma mutters half to herself, her stomach beginning to churn at the idea of two more people, two strangers, coming here.

"In bed, Emma, like the world's their playpen." Deede shakes her head.

"You gentle ladies are supposed to be on our side," Frankie says.

"No, my man, we are on their sides, a better place to be."

Emma scans the room. Jason's still staring at the tube. Frankie has his leg draped over the arm of her favorite beige chair. On the floor Rooster and Millie already lie spooned together. But she'd take it. Right now. Just the way it is. If only she could freeze them here for the rest of the day. "Everything's new," comes out of her mouth. They all look at her. They're waiting for the joke, she thinks. And if she knew one, she'd tell it, put them at their ease, especially Rod. But joking's not her style. Besides, their laughter's too close to hysteria to be real, and it makes her anxious that Rod will forget he's a normal, married man with responsibilities. A house, a wife, and more to come. It's what she wants, it's all she ever wanted.

Suddenly, Ida takes her hand, tugs her out of the room, though not before she hears Jason's whoop as he recognizes someone, God knows who, on the TV. Following Ida upstairs, she wonders if Rod will miss her. Probably he'll be relieved without her scrutiny. Tonight, though, tonight in the darkness, then he'll seek her out.

She pushes open the newly sanded bedroom door, pulls a small folding chair close to the window, where she can see the maple tree, the quiet street, the hot, white sky.

"They won't miss us for a while," Ida says, dropping into the rocking chair, stretching out her long legs until her bare feet rest on the bed.

"I was thinking the same."

"They may even calm down. We're their audience. We listen, clap, laugh at their antics. On the other hand, maybe they won't even notice we're gone."

"Ida? Why did you pull me up here anyway?"

"Because I can't believe Frankie parked his car nearly two miles from my place and wouldn't tell me why. We've never had secrets before." Ida raises an astonished face to her.

She reaches across to touch Ida's arm. "It was probably something stupid, something he didn't want to own up to."

"Maybe, but it's not the only thing. He's so restless. He can't be still long enough for me to feel he's really there. I need him to be a presence I can count on, the way you count on Rod."

Her eyes slide past Ida's pink toenails to the new king-sized bed with its wine-colored sheets and pillowcases, its snow-white comforter, its promise of a life she yearns for, one that is calm and certain, but already eluding her. She has the urge to share these feelings, but fears they might surprise Ida, whose eyes are already clouded with worry. "Do you and Frankie discuss marriage?"

"Who gives a flying fuck about fucking marriage? A fucking piece of paper."

"A piece of paper, yes, but there's a commitment behind it, too, a statement to the world that you're a pair."

"I don't care about the world. I don't want a house, ten beds, twenty windows. Just closeness and a lot of loving. Right now, there's too much empty bed. He's never there in the mornings. He leaves around dawn. Sometimes I pretend to be asleep, but when I don't, when I ask him to stay, please to stay, when I try to undress him, he peels away my hands, and he's gone."

"Does he make love to you?"

"Yeah, but not often enough. It feels like love, but then it doesn't. There's something between us, a kind of space I can't get past."

She wishes Rod would give her some space. Every night in

bed he clings to her. If she moves he wakes up. If she goes into the bathroom, he's sitting in the chair when she returns. She doesn't try anymore to coax him back to bed. "Anyhow, being together every minute doesn't prove love. Frankie would be lost without you."

"Then why does he need to be alone so much, Emma? What does he do?" Ida pulls her knees close to her body, wrapping her arms around them. "Once when I was coming off my night shift, I parked near his place. I had to know if he left his room as early as he did mine. I saw him cross the road and walk into Riis Park. I went in after him, thinking I'd surprise him, but he was gone."

"He ran off," Emma says dismissively, half afraid of where the conversation might lead.

"No. Gone. Like that rabbit that disappeared down the hole. He'd dug a tunnel somewhere to sleep in or keep drugs in or stolen goods or body parts. How do I know? God, I don't. I don't."

"Ida, stop. You just looked in the wrong direction. You know that. You're being silly."

"Believe me, there's nothing silly about it."

"So ask him what he does."

"You mean, 'take me to your tunnel'?"

"Tell him you worry about him, that you need to be with him more."

"That's how normal couples talk."

"You're letting him spook you. I think maybe you're beginning to spook me."

"God forbid." Ida suddenly covers her face. "Shit. I don't want to cry, but I'm angry."

"No. Scared, disappointed maybe. Women don't cry when they're angry." She reaches over to the bed table and plucks a tissue from the pearly white dispenser.

"What do they do?" Ida dabs at her eyes.

"Throw stuff—a sponge, a pot, even mashed potatoes."

"Do you speak from experience?"

She wants to say that's all she can do, but Ida's not really looking for an answer, not from her anyway.

"And there's something more." Ida leans closer, her voice a whisper, her eyes moist and frightened. "Something I pray is only temporary. He talks to an imaginary person. I've heard him."

Enough, Emma thinks. She leans out the window for a breath of fresh air, but there's only heat.

"Emma, it's like he's speaking to himself, except he's not, he's asking for agreement. Or approval."

Ida's words float around in her head. She doesn't want to hear them, deal with them, doesn't want to know what she knows, that much is wrong, that much is there to worry about.

"He says, 'Right, Papa-san? Okay, Papa-san?' "

"Oh Lord, what *has* happened to them!" comes out of her mouth as she drops back into the chair.

"Rod, too?"

"Of course Rod too."

"Oh God, Emma, I'm so sorry. I thought . . . well . . . he doesn't even drink as much as the others."

"It's why the house is so important. I want it to ground him, to frame us, to hold us together. Sometimes I wish it were constructed of steel and bolted on the outside, safe from everything." It worries her now to speak these thoughts aloud. Naming things can give them life.

"What exactly are you scared of?"

"I don't know. If I knew, I'd know how to protect him, us, from them. When I look out the window, what I see is what I expect to see. It's in here that everything's upside down. Every night he locks each window before we go to bed, no matter what the weather's like. He never says why. But something out there's threatening him. He doesn't want to be found. He's a fugitive. I can't stand the lack of air. If I say so, he accuses me of being too fussy. He tells me I need to learn to adapt. If I insist on opening even one window, he holes up in the bathroom all night, the door locked."

"Oh honey, none of this is good news. Does he talk about the war? I mean what he did there? Frankie's a clam."

"I don't ask."

Ida gazes past her. "Yesterday, my nursing class watched a surgical procedure. Everyone wore gloves, masks, the instruments were lined up. The abdomen was cut, held open with retractors, blood was siphoned off. It was intricate, detailed, precise. Everything mattered, everything counted. Everything was done to keep the patient alive. I suddenly wondered, what would Frankie feel if he were here? I mean he must've killed people, Emma. You ever think about that?"

"I try not to. But Ida, they had no choice."

"Everyone has a choice."

"Would you say that to Frankie?"

Ida shakes her head. "Do you think it's ungrateful of me to be complaining about him? I mean he's home with all his equipment, right. It hasn't even been that long, really. The war's still on, isn't it? Considering what they've been through, maybe talking to himself isn't anything at all. What do I know. I guess I can live with Papa-san if I have to."

"We're not used to them yet, that's for sure."

"And it's not all bad, Emma. The other day when I returned from work, he was there. He'd cooked this terrible meal. The pasta was mushy, the sauce was from a can he didn't even heat. But listen. There were daisies, my favorite, on the table. He bought a bottle of Chianti—just for me, he doesn't even like wine—and he'd drawn me a bubble bath. Now where can you find a man like that?"

"I know," she says, remembering. "It's amazing how sweet

Rod can be. He stood beside me in the furniture store, this beautiful man, and made me feel like a princess on a shopping spree. All I did was point and say, 'that,' and Rod informed the salesman 'she'll take that and that and that, wrap it up, send me the bill.' It wasn't this great event, just an hour in a store. But he wanted me to be happy. And I got the message. And I was."

"That's it," Ida says. "Take what we can get, all of it, whenever it's offered. Like camels storing water for the long haul through the desert."

"Except that Rod's embarrassed by the goodies we bought. He doesn't like being the only one to have them, so he's not about to keep an eye out for their well-being. I've been anxious about it all day. The men, I mean. I should be down there watching."

"What do you think they'll do?" Ida asks.

"Spill drinks on the couch, and that's just for a starter."

Ida laughs. "These guys won't waste a drop."

"And what about this Sean?"

"Don't worry, he won't be here, he's busy with Tess, although he does have a roving hand."

"He made a pass at you?"

"No, but he eyed Deede, God save him."

"Hey, is everything okay?" Millie opens the door a few inches. Deede pushes past her.

Shit, she thinks, the men are alone. She knows they should all go downstairs immediately. She closes her eyes for a second and takes a little breath. No one notices. It's her fate to lose all of it, bit by bit, starting now, and there's nothing she can do.

Deede moves nervously through the room, her hand skimming the comforter, the lamp, the table. They all wait for her, anxiety in the air. Finally, she turns to Ida. "If your brother continues boozing, he'll never get to the interview tomorrow." She addresses her directly, as if no one else were in the room.

"He'll sleep it off." Ida sounds annoyed.

"Hey, come on," Millie jumps in. "These guys need to break out a little. They'll calm down."

"Where's that written?" Deede perches on the edge of the bed. "There's something wrong with them."

"Says who?" Ida asks.

"Rod hasn't changed, has he?" Millie asks her.

She flashes a warning at Ida, then shakes her head. They see Rod as steady. That's fine with her. What's not said might just not be.

"You're blind," Deede says. "These men are all infected with the same weirdness. Even Nick. He hasn't shown his face since he returned."

"My brother-in-law is busy with my sister, Lucy," Millie announces. "Nothing wrong with that."

"Like pleasure is all there is in the world," Deede sneers. "But what about the bacon? Sooner or later they have to take care of business. If they want to get anywhere, that is. And here's something else. They don't trust us."

"What do you mean?" Emma asks, her tone low enough to be threatening, but nothing ever could stop Deede.

"We're supposed to be the other half, aren't we? So why are we missing? Ask yourselves that. Why are you never there even when you're in the room? I can't be the only one to notice, can I?"

"Don't be ridiculous. They can't be without us." Millie waves her dismissal, but Emma can see that Millie's unnerved, too.

"They do what they want whether we're there or not. We don't matter, not the way we should."

"Don't lump them all together, just because Jason gets juiced," Millie insists, her pale cheeks reddening. "Men their age drink, make love, and work. The excess wears off in time."

"Okay, then tell me who in this room sleeps well? Tell me that?" Deede's voice rivets her to the spot. "And tell me who isn't living with a stranger?"

"What're you so pissed about, didn't my brother marry you?" Ida asks, suddenly on her feet.

"The fact is, Jason's better off at home with me than here with them. They encourage bad habits. And you applaud their behavior."

"Well, then, let's send them back to war so we can keep our fantasies of the perfect life intact."

"I'm alerting you to trouble," Deede says.

"Just me?"

"I have your brother in mind, Ida."

"You have yourself in mind, Deede. If you want Jason to be crew-cut down to his belly button, forget it."

"He's out of control."

"I'll buy him a straitjacket." Ida peers into Deede's face from too close for anyone's comfort.

Millie looks to her for help, but she's worn out. "This is a party, remember? Let's not get so intense."

"Girls, girls." Jason tumbles into the room. "Don't hide in here. The men won't laugh at my jokes. I need my wife."

"Oh, God, you're slurring," Deede says.

"Slurring's in the ear of the beholder."

Ida smiles.

"It's not funny," Deede snaps.

"Here, baby, taste this. Three drops of white wine in lemonade." He lifts the glass to Deede's mouth. "Open." He kisses her cheek. "Now, drink it down."

"Slow up." Deede's hand on his arm.

"Can't. Have to live in a hurry, but not without you."

"Isn't that sweet?" Ida mutters.

"Why don't you help me, instead of encouraging him?"

"Now, now, I know I'm precious, but don't fight over me.

Besides, we need to hurry. Nixon's men are arriving any minute and we have to be there." He practically lifts Deede's birdlike body into his arms and suddenly they're gone.

"A drink, ladies, we need a drink," Ida says.

"I ought to dress the salad."

"What for, Emma? They can't taste a thing."

"Don't worry about the food," Millie says, "they're already into it."

"Shit!" She hurries from the room, their footsteps trailing her, drumming down the stairs. She could keep going, straight out the door, down the street, until it's all so far behind that nothing matters. Her fantasy's cut short by the raw cry of Janis Joplin: "Nothing left to lose. No, nothing left to lose."

"Where's Frankie," Ida's asking Jason, who's once more in front of the TV, a strange smirk on his face, the music rising to drown out any voices. Through the open window Emma can see Rod and Rooster sprawled on the lawn, passing a joint between them. Are they nuts? Stringy edges of pink bologna, pieces of wine-red salami, crusts of rye bread festoon the grass without the support of plates or napkins, a feeding frenzy in waiting for any form that crawls close to the ground. She grabs a garbage bag. Passing Ida, who's mixing drinks, she begs, "Help me get them back inside. The neighbors have children, for God's sake. They're smoking dope out there."

Ida offers her an inch of scotch in a plastic cup, but she brushes it aside—too little, too late—and heads straight for Rod. "They'll see you," she warns him. "You'll be arrested."

"The cops around here smoke, too, honey."

"To arrest you is their job," Deede calls out the window.

"Hey," cries Frankie strolling back up the lawn from who knows where.

"Let me guess, you met a man with a stash?" Rod passes the joint to him.

She collects what she can see of the half-eaten food,

searching for red-dotted olives scattered deceptively in the grass, knowing she'll never find them all as she'll never get through this day. She plucks the joint from Frankie's fingers, a stub so short and hot that she drops it involuntarily into the grass and then crushes it with her heel, grinding it into her beautiful lawn with a vehemence that startles her.

Millie yells from the window. "Don't any of you want to be in here with us? It's shady inside."

"The woman is wise." Rooster stands.

In the living room, Emma's eyes slide to the wall mirror in which she can see some of the men watching her. Rooster's already holding another joint. This time above her head, and he's grinning at her. When she turns to face him, he says, "Hey, gorgeous lady, don't dump the stash twice."

"It's his junk." Rod, too, wears a silly grin.

How many joints have they smoked? she wonders, watching her husband take a puff and hand it off to Frankie. There's less than a half-inch left, thank God.

"The last toke of the best stuff this side of the ocean." Frankie passes it on to Jason.

"Tastes like a compromise." Jason inhales deeply. "Stuff is light." He inhales again.

"Enough," Deede calls.

"That is a relative word," Rooster states.

Jason's using the TV as an armrest. Paper plates are strewn around his feet, potato chips mashed into the carpet. "You know what I think?" he says, his eyes wide. "I think Nixon's men know we have a beef with them and they're afraid to show up today. And they're right because we aimed our guns in the wrong direction."

"Eight thousand topics to chew on, why bother that one?"

"Listen to Frankie." Rooster stretches out on the floor. "Frankie knows."

"I hear you, Jason," Rod says.

"But he's not exercising enough brain cells. And the Lord taketh away what is not used."

"Jesus," Deede says. "Can't anyone talk straight?"

"A simple proposal," Rod states. "Declare the war over, who's going to care?"

"Nixon's men. They know the secrets." Jason spins the dial, one channel blurring into another.

"Take it easy," she tells him.

"Take it now, take it later." Jason snaps his fingers.

"Find him something else to play with," she whispers to Ida.

"Jason, come talk to me." Ida pats the couch.

"Right, you men don't notice a thing. The girls are back."

"Now there's something to chew on."

"What's this girl stuff?" Ida asks.

"Yeah," Millie chimes in. "We're ladies."

"Wrong," Rod says. "Ladies are rich. You girls are women."

"Damn straight," Rooster says.

Rod hands Emma a drink filled with several inches of scotch. She leans close to his ear. "Do you want me drunk?"

"Very much."

"Why?"

"You're too damn proper."

"If I wasn't, what would you want me to do for you?"

"I'll tell you later."

"Why are you two whispering?" Deede asks.

"Proper's the opposite of war," Rod states loudly.

"I second that," Frankie says. "And raise you one. I have bought me one big truck to move one big batch of crap for one big mass of people for one big pile of money."

"No shit."

She glances at Ida, whose face has gone all tight, her body straight back against the chair.

"It's true," he tells Ida. "You and I, girl—or woman—we're going to cover this side of the globe together."

"I'm looking for money, too," Rooster says.

"Count me three." Jason holds up four fingers.

"Do you want meaningful or money?" Rod asks.

"I sure as shit don't want one without the other." Frankie stretches out on the floor, propping himself up on one elbow. "Jason, since when is Jimmy Stewart one of Nixon's men?"

"That's Steve McQueen," Deede snaps. "You haven't been gone that long."

"This freakin' TV just fuckin' refuses to play the hearings." Jason grabs the scotch bottle, splashing some into Rooster's glass.

She watches the whiskey splatter the coffee table, hands a napkin to Rod, who places it on his head and gets down on his knees. "Lord, please help Jason find the men hiding in my TV."

"Hey, didn't we have some terrific times?" Jason flops onto the couch.

"Gone, baby, gone," Rooster chants. "Them good old hours of mud and fire, how tame the days to come."

"Man, how could Nixon's men send us there? I mean it was nothing I expected."

"That's right, Jason, it don't mean nothing." Rooster pats Millie's knee.

"Look, if the hearings aren't on, let's watch that movie," Millie suggests.

"I second that." Frankie sits up, tries to pull Ida toward him, but she resists, all color drained from her face.

"Go on," she tells Rod, "find the movie."

"No sir. We have to hear the man ask what'd he know and when did he know it."

"Wrong," Frankie says. "How did he know and how did he do it?"

"Right." Rooster holds up his glass. "Who did he know and why did he do it?"

"Amen," Rod intones. "Hey, what did they call you in Danang? Firehead?" Rod ruffles Jason's red hair.

Frankie salutes. "Jason? Sir! Request permission to reveal your name to group."

"Not granted, no way. Mention my moniker to these ladies and you get shaved, turkey."

"Yes sir! Request permission to whisper it to the men. Sir!"

"Permission denied and if you don't stop this shit, turkey, yours is going to be a whole lot shorter."

"Retract request, sir, name is now apparent."

"I have no interest in your sex-starved names for each other," Deede says.

"What did they call you, Rod, the savior with the black bag?" Millie smiles.

"Doc. They called me Doc."

"Tell the truth," she says.

"Morphine Minnie. But it didn't stick."

"Drugs, drugs, drugs." Deede shakes her head.

"No shit," Jason says. "What'd you do with that black bag of goodies?"

"Pick on him." Rod points to Rooster. "Man has no real name."

"True," Millie agrees.

"Second time around, I dipped the feather in mud and signed Rooster, comma, Rooster. No one blinked an eye. Then again, they were all wearing shades."

"Why did you reenlist?" Emma asks.

"First time was so bad I decided to do it over and make it better, but it just got badder. I already told you that, pretty bird, didn't I?" He touches Millie's hair.

"They're traitors." Jason jumps off the couch.

"Who?"

"Those suits with their winter and summer houses, traitors."

"Who?"

"Nixon's men."

"Being a traitor's not so bad," Rod says.

"Since when?"

"Since last year, no, year before that."

"Year before that what you did didn't matter."

"Four years ago I was a turkey growing all my feathers," Frankie says.

"You were a turkey that didn't know Thanksgiving was around the corner."

"Escaped the blade, my man, and be thankful," Rooster says.

"I considered deserting," Rod insists. "I don't know if that's being a traitor, but I did. Don't look so startled."

"Hey, man, that's the way I always look," Jason tells him.

"What stopped you?" Deede asks.

"I couldn't figure out the right moment."

Rooster glances up over his glasses. "Can't leave the brothers during incoming, now, can we?"

"Like none of you ever had your little fantasies. Not returning from R&R, or disappearing into Saigon, shooting yourself in the foot and getting your ass hauled off on some chopper?"

"My man, first thing I lost there was my imagination."

"And I couldn't run." Jason grins.

"I know why," Frankie says.

"Answer my question," Rod demands.

Frankie shrugs. "So we all had cowardly moments."

"Cowardly? No, man, that is exactly how I would not define it."

"At this moment I would say definitions are definitely not important."

"I mean, I *was* afraid, but that wasn't the reason."

"Listen." Frankie raises his hand. "Why refill our over-stuffed heads with this deep ancient shit?"

Rod crosses the room. "Deep-shit stuff is what it's all about, turkey, it's what it's all about."

"Yeah, but who needs it now, brother?"

"It's not a question of need, Frankie. It's all about where we'd be if we'd just fucking walked out of it. What the fuck could they do? Smart guys just vanished. Missing in action, my ass. Alive and well in Bangkok, better yet, they're pulling teats on some farm in Iowa. Name changed to protect the innocent. Jacobs is MIA, but Smith is happy as a pig in shit and he sleeps well, too. I think about that."

"Man was not a happy camper." Jason shakes his head.

"Leave the rock over the hole," Frankie says ominously.

"Why? Afraid of the truth?" Deede asks.

"Now, sweetheart, you weren't in that hole, so you can't know shit."

"Jason!"

"Slip of the tongue, slide of the word, sweetheart."

"Desertion is a private affair," Frankie tells Rod.

"Or you want it to be." Deede's voice is loud, much too loud. "Just shovel everything that happened into that hole you all know so much about. But if you men keep pussyfooting around in the dark, then we women are going to crash."

With a thrill of excitement, Emma hears Deede's gravelly voice, so odd from that small, stern face, those two glowing-coal eyes, and she wants her to press even harder, harder than she'd ever dare, although it scares her too. Because one of them, maybe even Rod, could explode, and then it would get ugly, and ugly is what none of them wants, what each of them is afraid of.

"See what a mess you stirred up." Frankie shakes his head.

"Yeah. This road leads to lightning." Rooster holds up his empty glass.

Rod begins pacing. Frankie throws an arm around his

shoulder, edging him toward the drinks. "Confession is not helpful except in someone else's church."

He's her husband. She knows she can't let it drop here. "I want to know," she says, taking some courage from Deede. "Why *did* you want to desert?"

Rod gazes down at Frankie's hand, then slides his eyes to her. "Two, four, a hundred reasons. But for right now the one outstanding was the lack of hot water." His eyes flick back to Frankie. "And I can't start a day without my bath. It disturbs the equilibrium."

"Just talk straight," Deede says.

"You mean get to the point. I tell all of you, there is none. There never was." Rooster sips his drink.

"Tell me something I don't know." Frankie laughs without merriment.

"Are the secrets that dirty?" Deede asks.

"They don't have to tell us anything, Deede," Millie says angrily.

"Yes, they do," Ida whispers, looking at Frankie.

"Jason here, he knows the facts."

"No sir. Wrong. Not me. Just never occurred to me to run away. I left the earth each morning and returned when my head hit the mat. A stoned escape, my sweet, dark beauty, and I'm forever grateful to all its unique possibilities."

"Great," Deede mutters.

"Oh, leave him alone," Ida says.

"Why should I? No one else here seems to give a damn about anything real. Don't make me the nut job."

"Well, sweetheart, I did have eight days in-country before learning the mysteries of a stash of hash," Jason says.

"I see it all." Rooster waves his hand at Jason. "Young, red-haired lad wanders along muddy road, meets charming sloe-eyed child who says 'GI number ten,' and hands over a little bag."

"Wrong. We're in the bush, it's nearly morning. We hear some branches crack. Everyone goes down. The LT whispers, 'Probably monkeys.' *Probably*'s not good enough for me. Then he whispers, 'You and Mike, check it out.' I'm not happy, so I say, 'Why? It's only monkeys.' "

Rooster laughs.

"The LT does the stare, you know, asshole low-life prick. So Mike and I crawl a few feet toward the noise, squat, and look around. More branches crack. Must be monkeys. I take out a cigarette. Mikey goes to visit the monkeys. Then, there's a flash of light, like the sun collapsing in the trees. I go down. Something goes down on me. It's the monkey, but I'm not moving, let it stay right there."

Jason takes a long swallow of whiskey. He totters briefly to his feet. "I whisper, 'Mikey, Mikey, the guys'll be here soon.' And they are. Someone says 'You're okay,' and I feel the monkey lifted off my back. I roll over. Mikey's head's next to mine, but the rest of him's gone. Someone hands me a joint. I take a long drag and never give it back."

"Hey, man, take a load off your feet."

"I don't take orders, not from anyone. I have mustered out." Jason slips to the floor.

"So you have, my man, so you have."

"Frankie," Jason says sullenly, "you stopped Rod's story, why not mine?"

"Drop it," Frankie mutters.

"No, sir. I deserve an answer."

"What's that supposed to mean?"

"We need to find us a dark watering hole without curtains where we can trade stories again."

"Man wants to slide the past off a high cliff, you got to let him," Rooster says.

"Is that it, Frankie?"

"You are stone drunk, Jason. Therefore, I do not need to

take your serious questions seriously. However, I will attempt to gather enough words to respond once. I have walked through the room, locked the door, and thrown the key down the rabbit hole. I will not, cannot, lower myself to retrieve it."

"That is a fucking intense statement, Frankie, and I didn't mean to get everyone intense. Shit, this is a party." Jason hoists himself onto his knees and crawls over to the TV.

"What you meant and what you did are two different events," Rooster says.

Jason begins switching channels rapidly.

"Hey," Emma calls out.

"Here, brother, you try." He snaps off the dial, drops it into Rod's hand.

"Oh shit."

"Coffee, we need coffee," Millie says but no one moves.

"Pull out the damn plug," she whispers, kneeling next to Rod, who's fiddling with the broken dial. He offers no response.

"Time to go home," Deede announces.

"Not yet, sweetheart. You and I, we're going to have a long and glorious night together."

"Then I'm leaving without you."

Jason grabs her hands, pulling her toward him. His fingers press her flesh so hard they leave white marks. The pain can be seen in Deede's face. "Dance with me," he orders.

Emma nudges Rod, who gives her a weird smile. Shit. No one's going to help Deede. She taps Jason's shoulder. "Let her go."

"She's mine, mine, mine," Jason sings, twirling Deede roughly.

Ida grabs him around the waist. He lets Deede go and they both fall back onto the couch. "Mine, mine, mine," he mumbles.

Emma's eyes slide to Rod. He's studying the TV dial with a

nothing-matters expression pasted on his face. She's seen that look before, knows that if she doesn't tread lightly Deede won't be the only one humiliated amid the wonderful new furniture tonight.

"Lord-y, lord-y." Rooster eases himself off the floor. "There's good news coming out of here yet." He climbs onto the beige chair, pulls Millie up with him.

"This wonderful woman and I are getting married and you are invited to the wedding." Rooster presses his chiseled features against Millie's soft cheek. Her lips force themselves into a grin.

"Don't move, you two." Rod grabs Emma's arm. "Where's the camera?"

"Try that drawer." She points to the lamp table, knowing it's in the linen closet upstairs, but not wanting to be sent away to get it.

Rod pulls the drawer out. "Empty. Shit, I can't find anything anymore. This place is too big."

"When's the wedding?" Ida asks, looking at Emma.

"The date?" Rooster nudges Millie.

"Winter. January."

Voices blast from the TV, although the screen is nothing but zigzag lines. If she could just pull the plug, but Frankie's collapsed right by the outlet, and he's wearing a don't-bother-me face.

"To the most beautiful couple in the world." Ida lifts her glass.

"My woman." Rooster wraps both arms around Millie's waist.

"A doll on a wedding cake." Rod aims a make-believe camera.

"A cover-girl bride," Frankie adds without much enthusiasm.

"Yeah, well, listen up, men, don't get confused. I'm the groom."

"Too bad, because we're going to dance Millie off her feet. Right?" Rod asks, jerking his face around in front of hers, so close she can't tell if he plans to kiss her or bat her forehead. She steps away, notices Jason lifting the last full bottle of scotch from the bar. Deede's eyeing him too, but she doesn't try to stop him.

"Hey, brother," Jason calls loudly. "A woman that pretty belongs to the world."

"Don't touch her, not even with your thoughts." Rooster smiles white teeth. "Or you'll receive the best of Uncle Sam's training."

"Can't imagine what that could be," Frankie mutters.

"I know, I know," Jason shouts. "KA-BOOM!" And flings the bottle. It hits the wall.

The whiskey drips down into an amber map of the States. Splinters of glass glint on the couch.

The noise remains in her head, shattering fragile hope.

"That's it," she says. "The party's over."

PART TWO

1993

AND AFTER

MILLIE

■ It's the night before Christmas Eve. Millie sits on a stool, alone in the Wantagh Beauty Salon. Out there it's snowing and a full moon lights up the sky. Instead of counting the day's receipts, she again steps down, again throws her jacket over her shoulders, again opens the door, and again stands in it staring at the nearby diner and the amber glow burning through its frosted windows. Her eyes slide to the decorations threaded across the street of darkened shops, then to the sky, and the perfect white moon with its snow halo.

Christmas is too big to fight. She still has presents to wrap, yet she lingers another moment, watching the snowflakes disappear into the snowbanks. When she sees the figure in the big coat loping toward her she quickly steps inside, closes the door, waits for him to pass, knowing he won't, wondering which forces, magnetic perhaps, damaging for sure, pull him toward her once more. She'll have to protect herself. But how? He peers in, his wild blue eyes land on her, and he opens the door.

She clutches at the wool of her skirt.

His teeth flash white and even.

She slips her hands into her pockets to bury her trembling, and forces herself to move behind the register. Her back against the glass partition, she braces herself for what has to come.

"Hey, baby, say hello." Shrugging off his coat, he sits on the couch. The coat lies in a heap behind him. He removes the wet plastic bags covering his shoes, tosses them over the rim of the wastebasket. Dark ribbons of water drip onto the floor and run between the tiles. Rod and Frankie have told her how he lives. Now she can see.

"Which way to clean?"

She points, staring at the coat, its soggy hem crusted with dirt. She hears the water turned on full force. Nothing delicate about Rooster. If only she'd left earlier. But he would've found her at Lucy's, and that might have been worse. Her sister's too fond of him, no, sorry for him. Probably both. With Nick as sick as he is, it's beyond her how Lucy has sympathy to spare. She wants the coat off the couch. It must smell and God knows what was in it other than him. People sit there all the time. Later she'll have to vacuum. And mop the floor again. Goddamn him. She flings her jacket onto a nearby chair. If she hadn't promised Lucy to stay here for the holidays, she'd already be in California.

When she looks up, he's coming back from the bathroom. His body still boyish in a crew-neck sweater, his cheeks sunken like some back teeth are missing.

"Hey, don't you talk anymore?" He fingers the combs in their cleaning solution, the brushes fitted into the racks, the smock folded over the chair. Then catching her watching, he grins. "Pretty Millicent." And ambles past her to slide the blinds across the front window. "Day's over, right?"

"That's none of your business."

"Whatever you say." His arms raised in mock surrender.

"What're you doing here?"

"Actually, baby, I don't know."

"I was about to close."

"Yeah, it's that time. Everybody to their houses. Fly away. Fly away." He smiles at her like she doesn't understand.

But she does. And she remembers everything, too. It's what he always did. Camp out, move. She refused, though, too afraid to find herself stranded with nothing but his love, a place to hold on to for short times that would never be a home. Wrapping a strand of hair around her finger, she glances at the clock. Five minutes, then she'll ask him to leave. He's a bad omen. "Listen, Rooster."

"Hey. Draw no lines on that high and pretty brow." He pats the couch. "Sit down."

She folds her arms across her chest. "I've told Sara-Jo about you. I haven't kept her in the dark." Even now she can see in his face her daughter's.

"That was right, Mil. Sara-Jo can't get anything from me." He cocks his head just the way he used to when she was angry at him.

There's no gray in his hair, no gray in his beard. "How do you do it, Rooster?"

"Same as the war. I manage."

"Don't you care?"

"Not anymore. Hey, don't worry, I like not caring. That's where I'm hanging."

She glances at his shoes, one laced with tan cord, one with black. "You could've sent us a postcard."

"Baby." He holds out his arms. "You have always been the only woman for me. I have never gone with anyone else since the day I set eyes on you. That's twenty years that no other woman touched me." He leans back on the couch. "Remember the bar in Queens, you couldn't walk anymore because of those heels and I carried you to the subway?"

"I was getting ready to begin my life when you came around."

He grins at her.

"It's true. Meeting you was a bad break for me."

"Yeah. I'm not good news."

"You can't sleep here. This isn't my place."

"No sweat."

"It's late, Rooster."

"You look better than ever, Mil."

"That and a buck and a quarter will get me on the train."

"How about a drink?"

"What's the point?"

"It's Christmas, baby. Somewhere there's got to be a bottle. And it's snowing. I need warmth."

He doesn't look like he's been drinking, but then with him it's hard to tell until it's too late. She shrugs. One, and then he'll go. He has to. She has much to do. She's got to visit Nick in the hospital before she goes. She owes that much to Lucy. Her suitcase still open on the bed, although her daughter's has been packed for days. From the bottom drawer of the desk she removes two plastic cups and a bottle of Johnnie Walker. Pours an inch into each cup, offers the drink at arm's length. His fingers circle her wrist, the ragged edges of his sweater touching her hand. "It's just me, baby. No matter what you see." His eyes ablaze in dark hollows.

He pushes aside the dirty coat, sleeve flapping toward the floor, and tugs her onto the couch. Then, retrieving the bottle

from the desk, he places it near his feet, and sits next to her.
He's wearing one black sock, one blue. She notices the shiny
worn fabric covering his knees, the long thin hand holding
his drink. The scotch coats her throat. Her eyes take in the
brightly lit shop. Tomorrow the women will wait patiently for
her attention. She'll cut and perm and dye and make them
feel beautiful. By day's end, she'll sweep up enough hair to fill
a large basket. His knuckles graze her cheek and she shakes
her head.

"Hey, I'm no stranger."

"Three years, Rooster."

"Just time, baby."

"You could've gone for help. We deserved that from you.
That you'd try something."

"Don't be mad at me."

"You didn't even leave a note."

"What could I say? My skin's too tight? I did what I had to.
Okay, baby?" He lifts his cup. "To whatever you want."

She remembers his silences, the lost jobs, his days of not
eating. Gone one week, home another. The final leaving had
to come. Pieces of him had been disappearing for so long.

"Hey, baby, I'm not your fault." One palm upturned, an old
gesture, the skin now hard and blistered.

For just a second she wants to massage it soft again. "To
whatever you need, Rooster." She drains the scotch.

And where will he be tomorrow? The day after? He has no
idea. That's what he wants. She shakes her head.

His arm goes around her shoulders, light as the plastic. She
smells the Dove soap. Everything is suddenly stark, recogniz-
able, especially the Christmas-green strip of rug that runs
from her feet to the rear door. California is big. Warm. Far
away. She doesn't want to watch him die. He can't make her.

His fingers massage her arm slowly.

After tonight, she'll never see him again. Because how will he find her? She looks at his face, this man everyone used to call handsome, his forehead lined, weathered, the dark, curly beard matted, the soft lips cracked. Only his eyes on her, still wide, bright, burning. It's hard to believe. Once his hands had searched every inch of her. Making love with him had been a relief from everyday life. A free zone in an ongoing war.

She slides off the couch, moves to the stool near the cash register, begins plugging numbers into the small adding machine, head down, not knowing what he'll do, never knowing that, even when she believed she did. Perhaps it was the hardest part, trying to see him the way she wanted him to be. Even now, she can't quite take him in as he is, worn and torn, because the other Rooster intervenes, like an extra membrane. She shouldn't have downed the scotch so fast.

"Mom?" Keys tapping at the door.

"Sara-Jo?"

Her daughter marches in, her usually red hair now royal blue. "Why is he here?"

"Hello, Sara-Jo."

"What's he doing here?"

"How are you?"

"What do you care?"

Stepping between them, she ushers Sara-Jo toward the back. He follows, lifting the Johnnie Walker from the floor. "Your hair? What the hell happened?" she asks.

"Why'd you let him in?"

"Answer me."

"Gail and I mixed some colors. I only wanted streaks."

Her daughter, not yet fifteen, dares many things.

"He can't walk in, just like that."

"Hush up," she whispers.

"Just look at him."

He's sitting in the adjacent cubicle, the scotch bottle resting in the sink.

"I want him out!"

"Take it easy, I'm not going to bite." He pours more scotch into his cup.

"Tell him to go, Mom!"

Her daughter's blue eyes, wilder than his. Somewhere out of reach is an answer. Only a mother can throw out a father. What if he won't go? What if she has to call the police? "He's only visiting."

"Big deal. If I passed him on the street, I wouldn't stop. Why's he bothering us now?"

"Hold on, girl."

"Why, what're you offering?" Sara-Jo peers back at him.

"Don't talk to your mother like that. I don't like it." He drains his cup, pours another.

"Tough shit!"

"Sara-Jo!" She pushes her daughter's shoulders back into the chair.

"Mom, he has no right here."

"He's still your father."

"I wish to God I could return his bag of scum."

"Hey girl, watch your tongue."

"Sara-Jo!"

"Why are you protecting him? He's not worth anything, the old drunk."

"Sara-Jo, try and understand."

"That he's crazy? Tell him it's too late. We're taking off where he'll never find us."

"What are you saying?" He stands, cup in hand.

"I'm not talking to you!" Sara-Jo leaps for the bottle, grabs it, smashes it against the sink. Scotch all over Rooster, the mirror, the floor, her dress.

"Sara-Jo!" Quickly lifting the top half of the bottle from her daughter's hand, she pulls her into another cubicle. Who is this blue-haired creature with a slash for a mouth. "Go home."

"I'm not leaving until he does."

Rooster, no longer grinning, starts toward them.

His sullen eyes bring it back. The years of her own silence, the fear of letting loose the violence beneath his easy manner. She steps in front of Sara-Jo, aware of the jagged half-bottle in her hand.

He stops, stares.

The backs of her legs graze Sara-Jo. She turns, face close to her daughter's. "Now. Go home." She means to appeal. A whisper. But her voice rises, high and unnatural.

Sara-Jo pushes past her. "No man's going to walk in and out on me. Ever. Period." The door slams.

A sadness she doesn't understand sends Millie's body against the wall. Sara-Jo has only one father, who's left her, and she won't be cajoled, won't acquire the habit of forgiveness. She watches him pace the adjacent cubicle.

"Get out, Rooster." She drops the bottle into the trash bin.

"Come on." He stops pacing.

"I mean it."

"You're chasing me?" Hands dangling at his sides.

"I want you out of here." Her eyes on a strand of frosty white hair curled around the leg of a chair.

"She gets it from you."

"Right now."

"Pretty Millicent."

"Just go." Lightness fills her head.

"Hey, baby, it's Christmas."

"I don't care." She hefts the trash bin toward the sink and begins picking glass out of the bowl. Silly to do it with her fingers. She ought to wet a paper towel. When she looks up, he's grabbing his coat. Once more the door closes, more quietly this time.

She leans against the sink. He's taken the plastic bags, probably dry now, like the dirty water on the floor.

Pulling the trash bin to the front of the shop, she slides open the blinds. It's still snowing. She turns away, tired of snow. Surveys the shop. At least another hour's work. Picking up the bits of glass, washing the mirror, vacuuming the couch, toting up the day's receipts. She'll mop the floor last.

EMMA

■ The vision's clear. A beach. No sun. Not yet dark. No people. Only she, wearing a long skirt, a blouse tied in a knot at her waist. No colors. Unless she counts the grays and browns, the black of the water. It isn't just here in the bathroom that the vision occurs. Sometimes it comes near the oven, or while putting away the wash. It doesn't matter if Rod's there or not. Even in unquiet times, when she's working in the office, helping one of the kids, or on the phone, it comes. What scares her is the absence of sound. Even dreams have sounds. She hasn't mentioned it to Rod, to anyone, although it comes more and more often and when it does, everything stops, or rather, she stops.

She sinks into the bathwater, letting it lick the ends of her hair. These few moments alone, she hoards them like preserves for another season. At Ralph and Angie's there's only a single bathroom. No one will be allowed more time than they need to do their business. She'll miss her kitchen, too. The girls will miss their bedroom. Rod and she will share Angie's pullout in the den. They'll have to wait to go to sleep because the TV's there.

In the movie *The Grapes of Wrath*, everyone watches as the Joads are evicted. Here in the North Bronx, eviction's polite. The bank will rent out their house for a year. If they still can't pay the mortgage, it will be sold. No fuss, no furniture on the street, no neighbors wringing their hands, no tearful relatives, no gut-wrenching photo for the newspapers. Just a quiet exit. Some suitcases, some toys. They could be going on vacation, not down the street to Rod's sister.

"Emma, I'm coming in." Rod slips in, locking the door behind him. He begins to undress. She lets out some water so the tub won't overflow.

"Beth and Laurie are asleep," he reports, landing heavily.

As if he had to tell her. As if he'd ever chance this otherwise, locked door or no. He's worse than her that way.

"Honey, stop worrying."

"I can't."

"It's just a temporary leave of absence." He begins to soap up her feet, massaging them as if each was unattached to the rest of her. It feels good.

The burnished color he usually carries on his shoulders is fading now that he's not working. She'd taken the girls to Yonkers to see him on his last job, high up on the steel girders, easy to recognize in his green felt cowboy hat. They were thrilled, but she hadn't liked it. Every second they were there, she feared he might lose his concentration, miss a step, drop a tool. She has a negative imagination, so he told her later, kissing her as if it were an endearing trait. It's just their difference. He refuses to recognize a disaster even after it's happened, while she's always on guard for what may come. Still, she tries to spare him. Real trouble can upturn his equilibrium and make him lose sleep to nightmares that follow him all day. She'd prepare him now if she could, but he won't let her.

"They're bound to start hiring soon," he says, half reading her mind, "and I'll be at the top of the list."

"How can you be sure?"

"Every once in a while they just stop building. It's not bad times. They do it so housing will stay scarce. It keeps the prices up."

"Your father say that?"

"Yeah, but I already knew. It pisses him off how little time they let us spend on each site. He says before Laurie's grown these new buildings will all collapse."

"What if it goes on longer than . . ."

"It won't. There's always more people and they need places to live, right?" His legs float around hers, his feet docked against her thighs. His expression softening. "Think about poor Rooster. Next to him, we're lucky. Besides if nothing happens soon, I'll rob a bank."

She watches his soapy fingers slithering between her toes. "Rooster's Rooster." She pulls her foot away. "And stop washing me, just listen."

"Don't I always?"

"Lately, you cut me off like a truck. What makes you think we could ever really move in with Angie? It's way too tight, and that's just for beginners."

"It's not forever, and we need that mortgage money for back bills. It happens. Relax."

"See? You won't listen. You're not even worried, but it'll be awful there. Ralph makes his boy say 'yes sir,' 'no sir' at the dinner table. I don't want the girls to 'yes sir' him. Besides, sometimes he wears his gun in the house."

"Angie's good, though, and she loves the girls and you and me, and she can't help who she married." He smiles.

"Wait until she washes your coffee cup before pouring you a second round. Wait until she makes you take off your shoes before walking on the living-room rug, if she lets you in there at all. It's true, Rod. It'll drive you crazy." No finger could surprise Angie's windowsills. Already she yearns for the lacy webs of dust that climb the far corners of her walls.

"Maybe, but no one else invited us in. It's free with Angie, so we can save almost everything. And she loves large families. I still can't figure why they have only one kid. She should've seen a doctor."

"Angie believes those decisions are made elsewhere." The ivory-pink cross that hangs over their TV comes into her mind.

"Maybe Ralph is the reason. He's the ex-marine. This is my weapon, this is my prick. He's forgotten which is which."

"You make light of everything I say."

"I want you to feel good, you know that." He gently lifts her chin with a single finger.

Startled, she peers into his eyes, now pale with passion. "Turn around, I'll do your back."

He obeys. Slowly, with the fingers of her soapy hands she kneads at his broad shoulders, instead of rubbing low the way she knows he wants.

"Emma?"

"No."

"Okay . . . forget it." When he quickly stands, the water drops to almost nothing. She slides down into it anyway, closes her eyes. And it's there. The beach. No sun. . . .

▪ Dry and robed, she tiptoes into the girls' room. Laurie's climbed in beside Beth, whose dangling legs she lifts back onto the bed. Even in this dim light, she continues admiring the wallpaper with all its pink roses, remembering the week of Sundays it took Frankie and Rod to put it up. Each time she spied a wrinkle, they pulled it off and began again. In the end, though, it was perfect and beautiful, a gentle print she's never become tired of.

Before she even reaches the kitchen, she's thinking about the fifteen pages she still has to type, already a day late, and even if she finishes tonight, it's still four days to get there and she may lose her place in some invisible line of freelancers. Maybe she can save time by mailing it from the main post office, and tomorrow's her day off.

She pulls the typing table up to the window, places the reports on the sill, drug reports for a pharmaceutical company. Sometimes the side effects listed are so horrible she has to stop and wonder. She used to phone Ida and read her the information, but not since Frankie's begun taking his medications.

"Momma?" Beth stands in the doorway looking concerned.

"What is it? Go to sleep."

"I can't. I keep dreaming bad things."

Go to her, she thinks, put your arms around her. But she has to finish. "Take some juice, then go to the bathroom. You'll be back asleep before you know it. Aren't I always right?" She focuses again on the tiny microscopic handwriting. She hears the fridge open. She can still get up, do it for her.

"Momma, don't you want to know my dream?"

"Tomorrow, tell me tomorrow."

"I'll forget."

"Then it can't be that important."

"But it is!"

She hears the tears welling up and stops typing. "Okay, tell me."

"I wasn't dreaming, I lied. I want to stay home with Poppa, tomorrow."

"No way, it's your cousin's birthday. Besides, your father wouldn't let you."

"He would if you asked him."

"Why would you want to?"

"I want to be with him. He's sad."

"He's not especially sad, just normal sad, like people out of work are sometimes."

"You're wrong, Momma, he's special sad."

She considers Beth's serious face. It doesn't matter whether she's right or wrong, if that's how she feels, if that's what's keeping her awake.

"Okay, I'll speak to your father, and we'll see, now go to sleep and no more thinking."

"Can I read in here?"

"I need to work."

"I won't talk."

"Not tonight."

"I can't read in the bedroom, I wake . . ."

"Read in the morning. *Please.* I have to finish." She wants to sound sorry, but it comes out annoyed.

She watches Beth place the glass in the sink, then bends over the handwriting. Does the child need to be with her now? Can one day make a difference? Is she right, that Rod's sad? Is that what the tub scene was all about? No, Beth's the sad one, a trait inherited from her mother. Rod's not worried. If he was, she'd worry less. Maybe. She isn't sure now. He can't love going to Angie's. Some people can throw a blanket over a tattered old couch and make a room look casual. Perhaps he's only making the best of it.

She moves away from the typing table. Only eight more pages left. She'll get up at dawn and finish.

She sheds her robe, slips into bed, her body close to his, one arm over his belly, her lips against the side of his neck.

"Ah, Emma, I'm so glad you're here." He rolls over, gathers her in to his warm body.

▪ She won't take the bus. She'll walk to the subway. In this heat, no one will be out, which suits her fine. She passes the pink-brick houses, narrow pathways between them. A few exhausted gardens. No front porches. Just decks out back. Rod wanted to build one, too, but fixing up the basement for the kids was all they could afford. He loves the neighborhood, the lack of traffic, the tree-lined streets.

She exits the subway at Thirty-third Street between Seventh and Eighth avenues. Mountainous piles of black plastic garbage bags seal off the curb. The sky's like milk, the sun hidden, the heat intense. A cluster of women, none talking, shake change in paper cups.

She tightens her hold on her purse and the manila envelope wedged under her arm. The check won't arrive until the end of the month. She's given them Ralph's address, but how long can they stay in a place barely large enough for one family that the girls don't even like to visit? Idle thoughts. Even if she convinced herself that moving into Ida's place would be better, she would never convince Rod to go to Long Island. They would have to change the girls' school, and when work did start up, Rod would have to travel more than an hour each way.

"Hey, lady, want to see a one-legged man do a jig?" The crutches thump rhythmically as he hops a circle around her, his head nodding to some inner tune of his own. Uncertain which way to move, fearful lest she trip him, she fishes in her pocket as he extends his hand, and drops—she doesn't stop to see how much—some change into the cupped hand. The palm does not withdraw. He smiles the wide lazy smile of someone who hasn't been given enough. "You enjoyed my dance?" he begins, but she hurries across the street.

It isn't fair to Rod's sister. It isn't fair to her. How will she and Rod ever have privacy in that odorless den?

"Aw miss, miss, gimmee something," a tiny woman whose face is old, sits propped against a brick wall. "Please, miss, anything."

She ignores the hand, the dirt, the germs, the bad luck they signify. Where else can they go? Friends listen sympathetically, but what can they do?

A baby asleep in the cage of a shopping cart. She gives the mother—legs bony, veiny, lumpy, sticks of clay that have hardened only in spots—a dollar. Her own strong legs always attract Rod. He tells her as he strokes them, and she responds in whispers. She'll never be comfortable making love there. They'll grow apart. It's inevitable. Circumstances can do that. She's seen it happen to other families. Look at Lucy and Nick, they no longer sleep in the same bed, or the same house. Poor, sick man.

In Sbarro Pizza, she orders a Coke while watching a man steadying a carton on his head pass the window. He joins a line of people dragging plastic bags of empty bottles along the sidewalk.

"Hey, pretty mommy, buy me a soda, too?"

She turns around. He doesn't look like the others. His khaki pants are pressed. His shoes have no holes. He wears socks. This must be his first day.

"Get lost," the counterman says, placing the Coke in front of her. She pushes it toward the man, pays, and leaves.

Even if Rod gets a job tomorrow, it'll take time for the money to add up, and there's only a week left in the house. What she needs is a miracle, but who can wait for that? Not even Rod. Angie's bound to talk Jesus to her girls, want to take them to church. Her chest tightens. She ought to sit down. But where?

She stops. It's there. The beach. No sun . . . The black water. She's walking toward the water. She can't hear it. Not yet.

Suddenly she sees the hand, then the red-bearded face, the cracked lips, the birdlike eyes, alert, distrustful. He wants something and she has nothing more to give. She turns to walk away. "Wait," he says. "Say no. Don't pass me like I'm not here." She says no, and wants to cry out "Leave me alone, go away," but the words stay layered and painful in her throat. His face disappears. She'd like to walk quickly, but the street's crowded and she has to thread herself through the maze of their bodies, mumbling "No, I'm sorry," "I'm sorry, no." "No, no, no, no," until she reaches Eighth Avenue, where she stands, perspiring, in front of the post office. Five men asleep, one on each step. No shoes, no shirts, their faces hidden against small bundles. Although people pass close to their heads and the traffic noise is deafening, they don't stir. They could be dead for all she knows.

She stares at their backs, tries to imagine them asleep as children, loved, like her girls. Surely, they must have had homes, apartments, once. She can't see even one of them hanging up his pants in a closet, pulling down the shades, getting into bed and falling into a deep dream-filled sleep. Their pricks must be unwashed for days, maybe weeks. How could they make love? They're finished. Discarded like garbage. A revolving door flings her into the post office, her heart beating like she'll never be able to explain it.

Rod will say it isn't their fault and it isn't her fault, forget them, don't go down there again, it's not safe, not good. Stay home, here. Yes, she will.

▪ In the kitchen, Rod's packing her typewriter. He's planning to move necessary things piece by piece. He stretches, reaching for the ceiling.

She opens the fridge for something to drink. It's there. The beach. No sun . . . Suddenly, the roar of the ocean. She drops the plastic bottle. The liquid spurts out, soaking her feet. Rod throws down a handful of paper towels. She's not sure if it's the ocean or her heart pounding in her head.

He's holding her hands.

"Once we walk out of here, we're never coming back. I know it. You just won't know it with me. You keep pretending the house is going to be ours again, but you don't get back what you give up."

"It's just for a while."

"They're telling us that so we won't make a fuss. I'd rather stay inside."

He puts his arm around her waist. "We're not going to lose it, Emma, this is America."

"Go downtown. Barefoot people dragging bags of empty soda cans, laying out their clothes on the sidewalk, selling them for a cup of coffee. Right here, not Calcutta. They were like us once, but not now, not anymore."

"Listen, baby, it's not the same. . . ."

"They were stupid." She grabs his shoulder. "They never should have left their homes. They should have barricaded themselves inside, stood guard with machine guns."

"Momma, you didn't tell him about Joel's party." Beth's staring at her.

"Joel? Who's Joel? What does he have to do with moving?" She lets go of Rod.

"I don't want to move either. I want to stay inside like you said, Momma."

"What the hell are you talking about, Beth!"

"I want to barricade the door. Please, Poppa. Listen to her, I don't want to end up on the street. I want . . ."

"Beth, stop. Your mother's a little tired, that's all. We're just going to be at Angie's for a while, then we'll move back in here. We're not even taking our furniture. Would I leave everything if we weren't coming back?"

"I don't know," she whispers, "but Momma thinks so."

"Come on," he says. "You've got chores in the backyard."

"Please let me stay."

"I need to talk with Emma alone."

Beth looks to her for help. There are things she must do first. Put back the curtains, especially in the living room. The bay window looks out onto the street. "I'll call you in soon. I promise, Beth. I *promise.*"

She watches him push Beth gently out of the kitchen. What if they do just stay? Maybe the bank will leave them be for a few months. She remembers reading about a black woman who didn't want to be evicted. The police shot her. If Rod wants, he can take the girls to Angie's, be on the outside, give interviews to the papers. If the police won't let him, he'll get Frankie, Sean . . . His friends won't let her die.

"Emma . . ." He's leaning against the sink, his hair ridiculously curly, the tiny garnet she bought him shining in his ear lobe. "You've had a bad trip, don't bring it home. It doesn't belong here with the kids. Forget it."

"The people down there, they're no age, just old, all of them, even the young ones."

"Baby, listen, we'll see the house every day, watch over it. I bet they don't even rent it for weeks."

She begins to unflap one of the empty cartons piled beside the fridge. She wants them all out of the way.

"We just need to catch up, pay some bills, and we're home again."

"You're right," she says. "So we can't pay the mortgage now, let them wait."

"They won't wait. It's the law. The bank doesn't want our house. They have hundreds of them, each one ten times better than ours. We're nothing to them."

She moves the flattened carton into the closet, takes out the ironing board. "Then you bring the girls to Angie's, and stay there until . . ." She leaves the thought unspoken.

She pulls a rumpled curtain out of a box near the back door, lays the ruffle out on the board. "All we have is twenty years' worth of this house. I won't give it up to a hope that everything will turn out all right someday." She presses on the curtain, but the iron's still cold.

"I never see you this way. I don't like it."

"I know."

"I don't like violence."

"I know."

He grabs her by the elbow. "Maybe I should get Frankie."

"Not yet."

"I don't like doing things hysterically."

"I know."

"I'm not sure what they do in cases like ours."

"Neither am I."

"They could use tear gas, smoke us out."

"It won't be like that." The iron, now hot, slides over the curtain.

"What about the neighbors?" He's staring at her.

"We have nothing to be ashamed of."

"It could get messy." His hands balled into fists.

"We have nothing to lose." Her tone matter-of-fact.

"You mean," he steps in front of her, "just don't move?"

She rests the iron upright, looks into his cold blue eyes. A shutdown, a lockout, a retreat to that place he runs the risk of losing his way back from.

"*The Grapes of Wrath.* Let's rent it on video tonight."

■ Darkness surrounds the house, making the light inside seem warm and welcoming. She sits on the couch. He comes in wearing fatigues. Her stomach clenches. "Where did you find those?"

He lowers himself down next to her. Their thighs touch. He pulls a red bandanna out of his shirt pocket, loops it around his head.

"Where are the girls?" are his first words.

"Why are you whispering?"

"Get them."

She finds them sitting at the head of the stairs. "Poppa wants you in the living room. With us."

She clicks on the TV.

"Mute it for a while so I can hear Frankie's truck."

"You called him?"

"Jason, too. And Sean. They'll park in front."

"What good will that do?" But she knows immediately what good it will do.

"They'll establish a perimeter, camp out. A tent in the back, another on the lawn. We need to secure the nights." Beth and Laurie watch him with eyes scared and. adoring. He turns off each lamp, rejoins her on the couch.

"Sit here," he instructs them.

The girls huddle together at their feet.

This was what she wanted, wasn't it? But he's gone so far, so fast. She stares at the silent, throbbing screen. "At least I won't see the beach anymore," she says to no one in the whole universe.

TESS

■ "You're not Nicole's father."

Sean hurried up Seventh Avenue, hunched against the snow, carrying the shopping bag full of Christmas presents. Maybe it was a stunt to get him back. It wouldn't work.

The wind picked up just as he entered Penn Station. A plastic wreath wrapped in dusty gold ribbons hung on the information booth. He went straight to Gate 17. The train to Babylon was already there.

Black rings of melted snow marked the aisles. The car was cold, the seats unseamed, the windows streaked with dirt. How long since he and Tess had even spoken? The first time he drove back to visit Nicole, there was a note pinned to his clothes on the deck, the cardboard box gone soft from rain, the clothing wet with mildew. "You can visit Nicole at my mother's. Don't come in."

A man crept into the seat across the aisle, and stretched out, arm over eyes, shoes protected by plastic bags.

The train moved slowly through the long, dark tunnel. He hoisted the shopping bag onto the overhead rack. He'd wrapped each gift in tinfoil. He didn't enjoy the shopping or the wrapping, but he wanted to give her everything.

The sudden white light was Long Island City. Usually when he visited he drove across the Triborough to the expressway, avoiding the dead towns that lined the railroad tracks. Even the sun didn't brighten them. A white dusting of new snow lay over the opalescent snow packed along the embankment.

"Tickets, please." The conductor stopped by the sleeping man, repeated, "Tickets, please," and walked on. He wondered if the man heard or if he was in that kind of sleep where even what you heard couldn't wake you.

He wasn't letting go of Nicole until she was done with him. But he couldn't go back to that tiny house with its fractured windows that broke the world into tiny pieces, or to the nights at Frankie's drinking bourbon until Tess came to take him home. Her strength always surprised him. Only when in a bar or on a long drive to the shore could he feel sure she wouldn't find him.

The man hadn't moved. He looked familiar. Maybe because he looked dead. He'd seen the dead. Astonished. Caught. On the bulkhead in front of him, a poster in the resplendent colors of summer, tanned guy, his peach-colored girl, amber beach, that throbbing pack of cigarettes under the curve of her breast. He hadn't slept all night. Probably looked terrible.

Pulling his jacket close, he peered out the window. Freeport. A clock rotated slowly on top of the gray factory. Across the street from the factory was the bus to Jones Beach, where he and Nicole sometimes collected shells on cold winter Sundays, where Tess told him she wanted another baby.

He never told her that he was afraid to try his luck twice, or why.

A low breathy sound. The sleeping man pushed at the air as if shooing away bad news. Sean watched him turn, his body curling into a fetal position, his head on one arm; the other, dangling, quivering a moment as the fingertips touched the floor, where they remained poised, unmoving. Nearby, a ticket stub from some play, maybe a concert.

He remembered the Rolling Stones concert. Tess couldn't stand the noise, wanted to leave. Actually he was glad to. The concert depressed him. Mick Jagger looked desperate up there. In the car, she accused him of killing her with silence. Why, he asked, did she need to know what he was thinking? He'd left the concert, hadn't he? At home, she whispered he only wanted sex to relieve himself, that he didn't even kiss her anymore. He'd jumped out of bed, found some dope in an old shoe box in the garage. Rolled a joint. It tasted rancid. He'd thrown the shoe box into the trash can, watched the sky lighten, the snow begin to fall. Then he called in sick and stayed in bed all day, listening to Nicole trying not to wake him.

They'd done a good job with her. She was the best of both of them. He'd always be her father. There wasn't a thing Tess could do about that.

The man moaned, opened his eyes, looked at him. "Yo, my man, anything extra?"

He took a dollar bill from his wallet, leaned forward. His eyes caught on "J. C. runs amok" scratched into the back of the seat. Jason Connors floated into his head. A regular one-man show. Always on the road. No one sees him, not even his wife. Maybe he'll look him up. After he sees Nicole.

The man met his hand halfway. "Thanks, I appreciate." The warm, deep baritone surprised him. He stared at the tense, black-bearded face, the glittering blue eyes that felt uncomfortably familiar.

"Sean Metcalf," he said, after staring too long.

"Leonard Rooster Barodin."

He hesitated. Chicken, Squeak, Wimp, Brute, Blackie, Arrowhead, Poison. It happened there all the time. But something else lodged in his head, something he couldn't quite locate. The name, he knew that name. He should've given him more than a buck.

"I was Sandwich, always hungry. Why Rooster?"

"My snoring."

"You weren't just now."

"Only in a bed. You from out here?"

"Used to be. How long were you in the city?"

"Too long. Too long. They pick us up in some of these towns, give us a bed. I'm about to make myself available. A place called Babylon."

"It's the last stop."

"So I heard." He glanced out the window. "Could be Siberia. Thanks, my man." He slouched down, his feet on the adjacent seat.

Outside, the snow was heavier, the sky a white belly. Soon, as darkness came on, Christmas lights would frame the houses.

"Yo, my man?" He was up again, facing Sean. "Ever been to Babylon?"

"Sure."

"I've been to Wantagh, but not Babylon. What's it like?"

"Bunch of stores, bunch of houses. Nothing to speak of."

"I just wondered"—he scratched his curly hair—"if they put up people right in that town or somewhere else. I don't need a long ride in a van. Maybe I could get off where the sleep's being offered. See my point?"

"Listen, the towns are close together, you don't even know when you're in one and out of the other. It can't be a long drive in any direction."

"That's good. I hate being cooped up. If something touches me, it strains my nerves. Not much I can do if another bum rolls off his cardboard onto mine, but a night or two of uninterrupted sleep, that's heaven." He smiled. His teeth remarkably white, even, clean.

"The places they take you . . . men and women together?"

"Well, my man, what can I say? I got enough trouble making it through with one corpse to care for . . . see what I mean?"

"I'm sorry."

"Nah, what for?" He waved him silent.

The train went through Bellmore, McDonald's visible through leafless trees. Behind it, the playground where Nicole tried the big swings. She was only five, then, pumping herself higher and higher. He shouted "Stop!," jumped for the seat, shook her slim shoulders. "Never, *never* swing that high. You could break your head!" She wriggled out of his grasp, threw herself against his chest with the abandon of a flat stone. They hugged each other tightly, rescued from a horrible possibility.

"What'll happen if you don't meet up with the van?"

The man's fingers drummed the seat. "Maybe get back on the train. Maybe not. No sense worrying. Just keep it together."

He wanted to know how the man got through each day. If, after a while, anything mattered at all. "I can't camp out anymore."

"It's all I can do." The man was gazing out the window. He felt the train slowing, stood, zipped his jacket, wrapped the scarf around his neck, felt the letter in his pocket, lifted the shopping bag down from the rack.

"Hey, my man, take care."

"Right, we made it out once." He waved, not looking, knowing that wherever they'd met before wasn't as important as where they could meet again.

▪ The old taxi moved cautiously through the snow, chains clinking. It all looked so familiar. The houses, the street, the trees. An imprint inside him stronger than anything out there. If what was real had changed, he couldn't see it. He saw only what he remembered.

Suddenly, he was afraid. What if Tess didn't let him in? She had to. He needed to tell Nicole about California. He'd buy postcards of the beaches. She loved the beach. He'd let her pick out the place she liked best, and take her there, wherever she'd be happy.

Snow blanketed the small front lawn. The curtains of the pale yellow house were drawn. No lights were on. The front screen was locked. He went back out the gate and around to the side door. The snow on the path, unshoveled, reached his trousers. He peered in the diamond-shaped window. Darkness. Trudged around to the back. The deck, too, was covered with snow. So were the branches of the large maple tree. He climbed the two high wooden steps. The drapes were drawn across the glass door that led to the kitchen. He knocked, then tried to slide it open. No luck.

Winding the scarf tighter around his neck, he noted the light in front of Deede's house. He walked to the gas station, two blocks distant, the wind blew icy snow into his face, chapping his lips. He was aware of the snowflakes sitting on top of the presents. They were getting wet, so were his feet. He never expected to be tromping around.

At the gas station, he stood in the phone booth whose door wouldn't close, and dialed the number of the diner. After the third ring, he heard the click and immediately said, "Aristotle? It's Sean. Tess there?"

"No."

"Didn't she come to work?"

"No."

"Do you know where she is?"

"No."

"Is Nicole with her?"

"I don't know."

"Fuck you," he mouthed into the air. It came out as a small white cloud of steam. He hung up. He ought to go there, make Aristotle talk, or tear up the place.

Back at the house, he pawed at the snow until he found a twig. He leaned the bag against the railing. It was sopping wet. He grabbed the handle on the glass door, pulling with all his might. A sliver of space. The twig, inserted, massaged the tiny tongue of lock until it receded, then he yanked the handle. The door slid open.

Pushing aside the drapes, he set the bag on the linoleum floor, and began to take out the presents. He piled them on the table, the smallest one on top. Backing out, he left the door ajar. Should he have waited in the brown leather chair until they returned? But what if they never returned?

He bolted down the steps, his heart pounding, and dashed across the street. At Deede and Jason's front door, he stopped, took a deep breath, tried to compose himself. He reached up to knock, aware that snow somehow had crept under the cuff of his jacket. Knocked. No one answered. What the fuck's going on? He knocked harder, pounding on it with his fist. "Jason, Jason, it's Sean."

Deede opened the door. "Well, Sean . . ." He watched her swallow the rest of the words, her face settling into a tight mask.

"Let me speak to Jason."

She glared at him ferociously.

"Where've you been? In a cave? Jason's dead two months."

"How?" A hollow word that crept from some recess inside his head.

"Truck overturned."

"An accident?"

"You tell me." She bit off each word.

He stared at her, wondering if this wasn't part of some plan to throw him off, wondering too, what to do if it was true because he sure as shit couldn't deal with it now. "Where's Tess?" It came out angrier, more demanding than he wanted. He saw her hesitate, calculate.

"I haven't seen her," she said too slowly for his taste, "but with this weather, who goes out?"

"What about Nicole?"

She stared at him with small, shrewd eyes.

"Hey, Sean." Kevin ran toward him.

He stepped inside, brushing her body back as if it were a dusting of snow, knelt, and opened his arms. "Hey, big guy. You been taking Nicole to school?"

"She takes me to school." He giggled.

"How come she's not home, then?" He wrapped his arms around the compact body.

"She didn't take me to school this week."

"Why? Is school closed for the holidays?" He was trying to keep his voice calm. He glanced up at Deede.

"Kevin, come here."

He pressed him closer. "I *need* to know."

She took a step toward them. He stood, lifting Kevin with him. "I'm not kidding."

"I haven't seen them in a week. She didn't tell me anything."

"You know everything." He stepped back, Kevin's head

against his chest, the boy's cool, smooth cheek somewhere in the palm of his hand. The cold poured in like a stream of icy wind from the open door behind him.

Deede took a step toward him, holding up her hand palm out, her voice softening, a faint smile on her face. "Don't worry, Sean. I'll make some phone calls. Just put him down. Maybe she's at the diner."

"I called."

"She could be with her mother. She might have said something about that."

"You're lying." His voice sounded strange to him. As if it belonged to someone else a million miles away in another land.

"Put him down, Sean."

"Not till I get Nicole."

"Don't be crazy. I can't give you Nicole, and Kevin has nothing to do with her."

"It doesn't matter. I need to see her."

"Listen, Sean, I don't know where she is." Her voice a flat whisper.

He stopped listening to that deceptive voice and watched her face. The skin tight around the bones. Her brows dark half-circles. Her mouth an open hole.

"You're all alike, every one of you. Fucking tanks running over anything in your way. You know what I hope? I hope she's fucking left the continent, and taken your child with her. That's what I hope." The words when they came pouring out didn't surprise him, nor did the venom.

He felt Kevin wriggling in his arms.

"Put him down! He's not yours!"

A few flakes blew in through the open door. The snow could pile up in the kitchen, drip into the basement. Tess wouldn't like that. He let Kevin slip to the floor. Deede took hold of his elbow. He pulled away violently, turned, and walked out. He heard the slam of the door behind him. That voice gone forever. And Jason, was he gone, too? He stuffed his hands into his pockets, glad the presents were dry, high up on the table.

He crossed the street, went around to the back of the house, up the steps, and slid the door closed, knowing she'd taken Nicole away from him to meet her real father. Someone who'd treat her mother like a queen and her like a princess. Somewhere warm, where it never snowed, where the schools were melon-colored, and it didn't get dark until late, where Nicole would have a jungle gym in the backyard, and Tess would never have to wait on another table, ever again.

▪ Snow swirled against the side of the diner and left raccoon prints on the windows. Tess sat in the back booth listening to Aristotle clap the lids on the coffee urns. Snow made him nervous. Maybe he'd hang up the sign and send her home. But he never closed, not even for Christmas.

She stared at the blankness of the paper. Picked up the pen she bought long ago at some school fair. She had missed the last one. Nicole swore there'd been nothing worth buying. Dusty old stuff, she said. It only made her want to be there more, like the other mothers. For Nicole. Only she couldn't mix, couldn't be casual, couldn't say "Merry Christmas" without crying, couldn't hear "Where is Sean?" without wanting to say "Dead."

The night he left, she stayed awake listening. After the second night, she understood. It wasn't a trip, but leaving the way her dad had left her when she was younger than Nicole. The third night she went to bed and stayed there. She can't remember now how many days, except that her mother sat beside her and talked till the snow stopped.

"That's the way of men . . . the lot of them. . . . They don't get to know you. They sleep with you, learn how not to make you unhappy, the best of them, but they don't get to know you inside, where you know yourself.

"Your dad, they sent him off to see Hitler and he couldn't stay in one place after that. It happens to men who go to war."

But she was Sean's life, was supposed to be. The first days after the marriage, he was so polite she couldn't stand it. Then he became restless. He'd disappear for hours, then climb into bed beside her. She'd slide her legs up and down his, letting her warmth spread to him. She was always afraid he wouldn't return. Until Nicole was born.

Carefully, she wrote the date across the top of the page. The pen glided like it was new. She had planned this since she saw the address on the card he sent Nicole. His place, where she wasn't invited. Now it was he who would arrive unwelcomed. Her house would be empty. The neighbors wouldn't know a thing. She would be gone, and so would Nicole. For two whole Christmas weeks. What would he think, then?

She glanced up at Aristotle. He was sitting as ever at the scalloped counter reading the paper. Nearly bald, thin, barely taller than her. Only a year older than Sean, but she couldn't see him young. Ever. Weeks ago she'd told him about this letter. The decision to write it had energized her, moved her in a way different from love and left a taste in her mouth that she could clamp her jaws around, a heat in her body against the cold nights of sleeping alone. The letter would be a knife in his throat.

"I'm done," he said, tossing the paper on the counter. "All ads. No news." He swiveled around to face her. "If we get customers, I'll have to cook. Rosario phoned. He's afraid of the weather. It's not accidental, the weather, he says, and I agree. The earthquakes in Japan—and this too." Sometimes his eyes belied his tone, but not now. She waited.

"Those rockets they send into space affect the weather. They should be banned. The customers complain 'Where was winter?' and now, 'What happened to spring?' No one makes the connection, and they don't want to."

She tracked his movements in the gold-flecked mirror. He wiped tables that were clean, checked sugar dispensers she'd filled. Sean would contact him. Ask where she was. He'd lie for her. He told her so. Last week, preparing for the breakfast shift, she'd called out, "Sean, rye up front." He'd brought out the bread. "Forget him," he said.

"Dear Sean," she began, feeling the words already there, just waiting to fly onto the page. The writing took moments. She covered the words with her arm as she wrote, not to read what was already said, just needing to get to the end, sign off. *Tess.*

When she looked up, he was watching her, elbows on the counter. "Done?"

She nodded.

"I'll mail it for you."

She stared at him. "Why?"

He came to the booth. "It's not important. What's important is that you get some sun at that beach, bring back a few jokes for the customers. You hardly remember their names, and it puzzles them."

"Did someone complain? You never told me."

"You were walking like the tiles were eggs and a word would be too heavy for you. Besides what would I say? That you've been moving on empty, that you forgot the Sweet 'N Low with George's coffee. That you put butter on Stachik's plain bran. They'll live."

She caught a glint of orange in his brown eyes, the gray hairs in the soft brown mustache, the shape of his full lips. She slipped the letter into the envelope, handed it to him. The lie was evil, but temporary. When Sean learned it was only a

trick, it'd be okay again for him. For her the loss was permanent. He'd taken the past with him. Without even turning
around. She wanted to explain to Aristotle. She wasn't mean.
But then she'd have to admit that something inside her had
been damaged.

She heard the thud against the door. Both of them leapt up.

The woman lay sprawled beneath a thick coat. "Tripped."
She coughed. They each took an arm, helped her up, walked
her in. She was breathing heavily, her face bound with scarves.
They sat her in the first booth. She unwound the scarves, her
large face red from the wind. Her gloved hands pressed the
table. Her body moved back and forth with each breath as
though she were praying.

"Mama, take some of this stuff off. You'll overheat." He
tried to remove the large coat, but the woman shrugged him
off and did it herself, revealing a big-breasted chest in a navy
blue sweater. Next she took off the woolly gloves, smoothing
behind her ears the long white strands of hair that had worked
loose from a braid wound around her head. She wore one
dangling feathery earring.

"Take off your wet boots," he ordered.

The woman offered up her feet. He knelt, pulled off each
boot. Gently. "Stay here." He disappeared behind the counter.

The woman seemed to be studying her hands on the table.
What was she waiting for? Tess had no idea.

"So, Mama," he said, "what brings you here on a day like
this? Must be important." He placed a bowl of soup on the
table.

"Cigarettes," she said hoarsely. "At the motel they don't let
me smoke. I had to have one. If it weren't for the weather I
wouldn't be there, but I can't sleep in the snow."

Tess took some quarters out of her pocket, fed them into
the machine. She knew the motel. It wasn't far.

The woman barely nodded her thanks, lit a cigarette,

leaned back in the booth, and puffed gently, the smoke whirling toward the light of day.

"I have no money." The woman fixed blueberry-black eyes on them.

"Who does these days," he said.

She stubbed out the cigarette. He handed her a spoon. "Go on," he urged.

The woman blew at the soup then sipped it slowly.

"You're our first customer today," Tess said, embarrassed to be watching. "Did you walk all the way?"

The woman nodded. "Not fast. But not stopping. That's the trick. If you stop, you freeze. You've got to keep going in this weather. That's the trick." She paused, breathless, took another spoonful. "I know a lot of tricks about snow." She left the spoon in the bowl, lifted her hand, big like a man's. "You do this even with gloves on." She opened and shut her hand. "You keep doing it, pump the blood back to the heart, and keep your nose covered."

This said directly to Aristotle.

"It's different in the heat. The trick in summer is your feet. Keep them out of shoes and socks." She looked at each of them, then began again to slowly spoon the soup into her mouth. The redness in her face was gone, leaving the skin ashen and faintly yellow.

"There are lots of tricks like that. If you know them, the weather doesn't matter. Except to sleep. You can't sleep in the snow. No matter what you're wearing." She placed the spoon on the table, looked into the bowl.

"It's the only reason I went with them. They came in a van. I asked, where are you taking me? I like to know the address." She looked up, her gaze inward. "They said where the motel was. I thought, why not? I knew the diner was here. I know the area. If I'd had cigarettes, I'd have hidden them. That was the problem. They got me before I could get some to hide." She tipped the bowl toward her. It was nearly empty.

Tess nodded, suddenly sad. Then Aristotle's hand covered hers, pressing lightly. He'd never touched her before. His fingers sent warmth through her arm to the very knob of her shoulder. Should she turn her palm up? Into his? Send him a message that it was good? Didn't she want to stay away from all that? From those who would take advantage? But he wouldn't. If only she could turn and see what he knew of this moment, but it was too awkward, the three of them sitting so close.

The woman had spooned out the last drops, picked up the bowl and placed it at the edge of the table. She took out another cigarette, sighing deeply.

The hand was gone. She turned to see him leaving with the empty bowl.

"What'll you do now?" she asked the woman, and herself.

"Go back there till the snow's cleared. My friends are somewhere. I need to find them."

"Maybe they were picked up, too."

"Could be." She yawned. "Didn't sleep last night. No pillows. Can't breathe when I'm flat. Kept me awake thinking about a cigarette."

He placed a full bowl on the table, then sat next to her, their thighs and forearms touching. Sometimes they would drink coffee together at the end of her shift. But always they had sat at the counter, an empty stool between them.

The woman laid the lit cigarette aside. Took a spoonful of soup. "Did you cook it?"

"From a can."

"Tastes good when you don't have to make it yourself. Eating till you're full's another trick. Same as drinking liquor. If you need to sleep fast. Eat a lot." She left the spoon in the bowl, leaned her head back against the booth. There were red patches now on her pale cheeks.

"Are you okay?" Tess touched the hot hand balled into a fist.

"A little warm from the soup. I need to rest."

He turned to her, his face close, studying hers.

"The couch in the lounge," she said softly because he was a breath away from her words.

"I have blankets in the car." She nodded, but he didn't move. She turned toward the woman, the red patches were a flush, disappearing into the white of her hair. "You might have a fever. I'll get some aspirin."

"No pills. Maybe tea with some whiskey. A little nap. That's all I need." The woman leaned forward, breathing heavily, her voice low and hoarse, her hands massaging her arms, her eyes dark, wide, alarmed.

"I'll get the blankets."

She watched him pull his jacket from the coatrack and pocket the letter.

The woman closed her eyes.

"Hey?"

"Resting," the woman whispered. "It's good to close your eyes when you're resting."

She saw his boots under the coatrack. He'll have to walk to the corner, mail it there. Maybe he won't. Maybe he hopes she'll come to her senses. He has such good sense himself. That's always been clear. What hadn't been clear was that the warmth from his body could reach hers.

She went to the counter, poured some tea. Once, in a moment of high love, she'd thrown her arms around Sean's waist, catching him off guard, pulling him down on top of her. He'd rolled away, annoyed. Told her she didn't know her own strength. He didn't like being surprised by her love. He needed it to be quiet, uncelebrated. She'd learned that, hadn't she?

Outside in the swirling snow the day felt quiet, contained. A car inched by. She wished he'd hurry back. The woman's chest rose with each breath. What if she died? "I made some tea," she said, placing the cup carefully on the table.

The woman opened her eyes. "I was dreaming. Riis Park. Last summer. I take each season as it comes." She sipped at the tea. "Whiskey would help."

Across the street, H&R Block was shuttered. Deede wouldn't care, she was tired of her job there. Deede had been shocked when Sean left. She thought of him as the perfect father, the one Kevin never had and now never would.

"Mama, we're going to make you a bed," he said, stamping his feet, holding the blanket beneath his open jacket.

Tess followed him, strangely excited. It was out of her hands now. "Is she asleep?" In the lounge, he spread one blanket on the couch for a sheet.

"Just resting. She looks ill." She folded a second blanket for a pillow, tucking it under the arm of the couch.

"I could drive her back to the motel."

She could hear that he didn't want to. Neither did she. The woman's presence was a magnet. "Not yet." She went out, brought back her coat, placed it under the blanket-pillow to make it less flat.

They worked quickly. At least they'd get her into a comfortable position, stretched out, not too warm or too cold.

She watched him tighten the sheet-blanket, smooth out each wrinkle. It could have been for a lover. He stood back to survey the couch, which no longer looked like itself, but not like a bed either.

The woman shuffled into the lounge and sat down, her stocking feet planted on the tile floor, her hands pressed against her thighs. She coughed. "I left my cigarettes . . ."

He went to get them.

"Here, put your legs up, lean back, tell me if it's too flat."

She would do right by her. It was important. He placed the cigarettes and the ashtray on the floor.

The woman's eyes were deep, feverish. "It's comfortable." Her voice so low they bent to hear. "I'll rest." She placed the side of her head against the makeshift pillow.

He leaned over. "Mama, we'll be out there."

"Leave on the light."

The woman's boots were under the table.

"I can almost hear her breathing out here."

"We can always take her to the hospital." The back of his muscular shoulders reflected in the mirror.

"She might sleep for hours."

"She might." His skin still ruddy.

"You can't leave her here alone."

"We won't." He was watching her, his hands in his pockets.

"You mailed the letter?"

"Of course. What now?" His eyes steady.

"I don't know . . . that's it, I guess."

He slid into the booth, patted the seat. She slid in beside him. The snow was higher now than the wheels of the parked cars and still falling.

"Have you ever been to war?"

"No." He put his arm around her.

"What if we get a customer?"

"The door's locked."

■ He pushes past the curtain of noise, swaying a little. Phone's in the corner. Real old-fashioned wooden booth. No door, no secrets either. So what? He uncrumples the piece of paper in his fist, dials Pauli's number. Somewhere the staccato voice of Suzanne Vega, accusing the men in her life, hammers at his head. He'd better drop a few quarters in that box, find something he'd enjoy, maybe Ol' Blue Eyes or even Ella.

He listens to the distant ringing. Is she there at all? Probably not. Probably left yesterday, right after he called. Twenty years is a long time. A man could become a killer, a drunk, a grandfather. A man could stop being her brother.

Suddenly he hears her voice.

—Hello? Pauli? Frankie.

—No, not lost. I've got it all mapped out.

—Maybe thirty miles or so, I don't know.

—In a bar.

—Just resting.

—What? I can hardly hear you.

—No, don't bother. I rarely eat.

—Wrong? A man stops in a watering hole is all.

—Do I? No one's told me that before.

—I'm sure of the directions.

—Okay. See you soon, too.

His sister's voice strange, sharp, definitely not a kid's anymore. Shit, the pills are playing a symphony in his head. When he steps out of the booth, the smoke nearly chokes him. The place is dark. A few green-shaded bulbs dangle over a small, horseshoe-shaped bar crowded with men. Spindly-legged tables with quarter-sized tops are so close together it's hard to maneuver and the floor feels wavy like wet sand at low tide. He could ask Pauli to meet him here, because, truth is, the sun bothers him now and he's glad for this wood-paneled shade. And why's he going anyway? Well maybe he's not, maybe he'll just stay put and get drunk.

He makes it to the bar. Either the bartender's grown taller or . . . Fuck it, tomorrow he's dropping the pills down a sewer, the blue ones too. And the hell with vitamins and minerals, so many each morning his head reels just counting them out and his throat feels like it's been flattened by a steamroller. The hell, too, with sleep or no sleep, or caring about either. And, Papa-san, we're definitely going to have us another drink. Whatever's left is going to be quality, and taste good, too. "A Sam Adams drawn slow from the tap," he tells the bartender, his eye caught by the silver glint of dog tags. He looks up into the narrow, caramel-colored face. He refuses to believe it. He drops into a chair at a vacant table and takes a long swallow of his beer. It can't be. The cold bitter sweetness slides past his tight throat. It simply can't be. He blows out the candle flame flickering in its tin container. A thin spiral of smoke disappears into the haze. He might bum a cigarette. Pauli used to smoke. Pauli. Does he even want to know about her anymore? A widow alone on some rural road. That he does know. Woods that'll probably freak him out. Sure as shit she won't recognize him. Not him, Papa-san.

His eyes flick back to the man. It can't *be*. Slim brown arms sprout from a green T-shirt. That same pointed chin, wispy beard. J. J., who partied inside his track many a night. Preachiest drunk he ever knew. But J. J.'s dead. Maybe this bar's filled with dead people, the last stop before the great divide, or maybe this *is* heaven. Except he had to lay down cash for beer. Not right, Papa-san, the tab on that trip should be prepaid. Fuck these pills. J. J. wouldn't want to be bothered by the likes of this white guy anyway. Not anymore. Not after all these years. Still, he can't help himself, can he? He pulls the baseball cap lower on his too-shiny head and begins inching his way toward the bar.

"Jones?" He hears the hesitation in his voice.

The man's body stiffens with annoyance.

"Frankie Bower, Trackman, second battalion, Danang, 'sixty-nine."

Eyes slide up him, computing the evidence. "Yo, stud." J. J. jumps off the stool, throws a long arm over his shoulder.

"Someone saw your name on the wall," he complains.

"Most overused slave tab in the army." J. J. slaps his chest. "Intact. Almost. What are you drinking?"

"A beer at a table over there."

J. J. follows him, spidery fingers clasping a whiskey glass. "So how you doing, eh? . . . Trackman, right?"

"Maybe my name's on that wall, too." The second beer has loosened his tongue.

With one swallow J. J. empties his glass. "Wall, my ass. Chickenshit scratchings on granite." J. J.'s wiry torso leans toward him. "You one of those gung-ho vets? Parades, medals, all that shit?"

"Just living. Right, Papa-san?"

"Papa who?"

"Old friend. Fellow traveler. My Tonto. Papa-san, meet J. J." His voice is hoarse, his head feverish. He takes a swallow of the beer just for the coldness it contains.

J. J. cracks a smile. "Pleasure's all mine."

"Papa-san's my hugger, my cloak, my yoke, my responsibility, the sight in the back of my head."

"Yo, man, now we're singing. I left my hugger there and I've been yearning ever since. Which side was he on?"

The kind of question Pauli would ask if he introduced her to Papa-san, which he wouldn't, because she'd let him know that everything she ever feared happening to him had happened. "Both," he says emphatically.

"I knew some VC myself, that surprise you?"

"A little."

"Well, Trackman, surprised me, too. But it didn't last long because good things pay no salary and so I ended up right here in the Bronx Post Office, most boring job in the world."

"I bought a truck, moved furniture coast to coast," he says, relieved to drop the subject. "Finally, I gave it to a friend." Jason accepted it with both hands, he remembers, but Ida hated the idea. She thought it meant he'd given up hope. Hope, something that belonged to the rich, the poor, the religious, the stupid, the naive, but not to him, not for twenty years now.

J. J.'s eyeing him suspiciously. He wonders if he's missed something. Perhaps some words to tell him that J. J.'s body is filled with warm blood the way that Jason's is no longer.

Dumb fuck rolled the truck over and over like a goddamn ball. Mashed and smashed. Dead. What a gift.

"Too much time to think, right? That's the killer that sent me into OD. Everyone thought it was stupid, but stupid people don't kill themselves, they go on living."

Now J. J.'s reading his mind.

"Ever been to the top of the Bronx before?"

"Sure. VA clinic."

J. J.'s eyes fasten on him. "Why'd you slosh through those hallway trenches?"

"Leukemia."

"Agent O, the agent of C, the one that seeps through your boots, sits in the skin between your toes, waits like Santa Claus to see if you've been naughty or nice. You've been bad, Trackman." J. J.'s arms shoot across the table. "Shit."

"That's what I say."

"Right, Trackman." J. J. turns profile. "Bastards ruined a country, poisoned their own, and never got nailed for it. I say that's a sin. I tried, though, I sure did. Like Papa-san here, he tried too, didn't you, Papa-san? That's right. We did some damage, me and Papa-san. We attempted to rectify the dirty deeds."

"That was a long time ago," he says, suddenly exhausted.

"So was slavery. But it happened." J. J.'s eyes burn the room. "Mind you, I didn't carry no flowers. I was armed with firsthand experience and Uncle Sam's MO." He drains the whiskey glass. "Let's buy you another drink."

"Sam Adams," he says, pushing a bill under J. J.'s hand. He watches J. J. shoulder his way through the crowd. Meeting J. J. could be a sign that he ought to stay home, because something big is waiting here to make his final exit a show of shows. But he doesn't believe it. Because J. J.'s presence is one clear reminder that nothing here is as important as making the journey there. That if he is heading in the wrong direction, it must be to Pauli's. Because what's the point of traveling the past with her? Why drive thirty miles to sit in some room and resurrect what was buried so long ago? Especially if he plans to put this side of the ocean behind him?

The drinks have deadened the pain that usually squeezes his joints. Only his brain is still spinning, and at a pace that's making him dizzy. Not to worry, Papa-san, no more pining, no more whining, you're going home.

J. J. sets a beer in front of him, straddles the chair, and begins drumming his long fingers on a napkin.

Of course it's J. J., a little more nervous maybe, but him and no one else. "Still wearing the tags?" he asks, because they annoy him, sashaying across the man's chest.

"They remind me of who I am, and what I did. Hey, Track-man, how many VC did you kill?"

"Jesus, come on, who knows."

"Just did it in the dark, right? Could've been anyone, or anything. Quick fuck. Never made a sound."

"Enough," he says, his hand balling into a fist beneath the table. Why is J. J. peeling his skin this way?

"Could've been me." J. J. downs his whiskey in one fast gulp. "Listen, man, the U. S. Army never paid me enough for that kind of blood. Get it? Kill for the Mafia and you live in splendor. Kill for Uncle Sam and he mails you a disability check."

"J. J., I've got a mess to think about without you dropping these pearls of shit on me, see?"

"What I see is a man my age, which is no age to carry such a load. Dig? Now's the time for ease, the time to leave the slippery slope, to be eye level with the whole scene."

"If I knew what you were talking about I might listen, but you've neglected to fill me in."

"Trackman, you are filled in so tightly, you're sinking to the bottom. I'm just trying my best to lighten the density. Another drink?"

He shakes his head, but J. J.'s already moving swiftly through the crowd. The man's bombed. He'll end up having to bed him down. He should just get out of here before the shit hits the fan. He slides between tables. Someone's just leaving the phone booth. Lucky him. He dials, listens to the ring. She could care if he didn't show up, her crazy brother who could rip up her place, her life.

—It's me. I got hijacked by a friend.

—Right. Still in the bar.

—I haven't seen him in years.

—What? Just a couple of beers.

—It takes more than that.

—I could drive with my eyes closed.

—Why would I do that?

—No, I'm not harassing you. Just being polite. It's rude to arrive late.

—Yes, I'll be there. What's the matter? Don't you like talking on the phone?

—Well, sometimes you have to.

He hangs up, returns to the table, digs a pen out of his pocket, writes his name and phone number on the driest corner of a napkin, then wends his way toward the bar. "I have to take off," he mutters, laying the napkin on the counter.

"Aw, man, you just found me." Something in the man's voice snags him, fills his mouth with the taste of damp nights, hot mornings. "You thought me dead, right?"

He nods.

"I'm the message, not the messenger, understand? Give this man another Sam Adams."

He allows J. J.'s hand to guide him back to the table.

"Tonight's special, Trackman."

"If you say so."

"You and Papa-san were looking for me."

He wonders if J. J.'s right, if his was one of the faces he's been reviewing on the backs of his eyelids for weeks? "Why would we do that?" he mumbles.

"Unfinished business. Truth is, you saw the tags, you saw the 'Nam, right? Natural, that's natural. Then I tell you how I was friendly with some VC and you tell me you have to take off. What am I to make of that?"

"Anything you like."

"If you hadn't come in here today, you'd have me buried. But now you've dug me out of the ground, so deal." J. J. squares his shoulders.

"I'm finished dealing. It's over, done, just like the war, understand? And I'm due at my sister's place."

"Sure." J. J.'s liquid eyes hold his own. "Connection's good. Keeps us from being alone with the hairy problems to tickle our asses, right?"

"If you say so."

"We share memories, Trackman."

"You're one drunk preacher."

"I'm the missing piece of the pie, the sliver of glass that fills in the window. That's why we met today. So you can't leave."

"I told you I have to visit my sister. I last saw her the night before I left for the army."

"And you'll never see me again." J. J. tilts his head. "I'm your accident, your arbitrary encounter, you can't repeat me."

"Say something I understand."

"Check out the wall again."

"You're here, you weren't killed."

"Trackman, where they going to write your name? We've been falling down dead for twenty-five years. No walls for us.

We made it out, we just never landed. So you call your sister, tell her not to light the flame under the pot just yet. Say you're with J. J., one dead man walking around drinking whiskey. You need me, Trackman. It's hard to know alone if what you remember is what happened."

"Ride up with me then." The idea hits him after the words are out of his mouth. He and J. J., together again on the road. That appeals to him.

"You want to introduce me to your sister?"

"She shares your philosophy on the war."

"Tell her there's room at the table." J. J.'s foot pushes out a chair.

"It's too late."

"Not till they close your eyes. Invite her down. You wanted me to meet her, or is she too white to come here?"

"Listen, for all I know about my sister she married a black guy."

J. J.'s mouth slides into a sneer. "She didn't."

"Well, she's got a lot in common with you anyway."

"Is that a fact?" J. J. moves both empty glasses into the middle of the table. "You buy, I fly."

He extracts a ten-dollar bill from his wallet, gives it to J. J., who's already on his feet. Then he presses his hands on the table to steady them. Soon he won't be able to navigate a straight line out of here. We'll get there, Papa-san. The night's long. The life's short. Actually he wouldn't mind spending a few hours sinking into Ida's big feather bed, the softest place in town. Keeping her body warm is his job, although he's forever pulling back the top sheet so it can't wind around his legs like a shroud. Now she's a good memory, Papa-san.

J. J. sets down their drinks.

"Well," he says, "will you ride up with me?"

"No booze, no prose."

"My sister'll have a bottle. Right, Papa-san?"

"Papa-san knows all." J. J.'s eyes search the room.

"What're you looking for?"

"Information, Trackman, information."

"You're drunker than a lord. A ride will clear our minds."

J. J. shakes his head. "Forget it, my man, there's not enough time to fill them again."

"You rode my track day and night, remember?"

"Does it matter?"

"Everything matters." His head's pounding again.

"I see in you what you see in me."

"No more riddles."

"Right. One lifetime just isn't enough to understand everything. That sucks, man, doesn't it?"

"Ride up with me now."

"I don't think so."

"You want an engraved invite?"

"The other side, man, I joined the other side." They stare at each other.

"What're you saying."

"The other side, that's right."

NVA? VC? A fucking traitor? "Why'd you do that?"

"Insurance, Trackman, insurance I'd get into heaven."

"You shot at us?"

"Nah, I just gave them blankets, a few bandages, morphine, a handful of pills, yeah, even a pile of fatigues. No guns, though. Couldn't count on them to work anyway."

What's he supposed to do with *this* information? Slap J. J.'s hands, walk out? The truth is, he can't even detect a speck of anger. "There is no other side, not anymore," he surprises himself by saying. "And anyway, I plan to walk light, eyes open, shake some hands in the villes, explain a few things that've been rolling around in my head since I left." That might get rid of the buzzing sound clogging his ears so that when he finally does lie down he'll be able to hear the big red ant scratching up the leaf the way he did the first week in country. He still wonders what else he's stopped hearing.

"Trackman, I'm renaming you Riddleman, because my wires are not picking up your meaning."

"Come with me tonight," he repeats.

"I can't. I'm out on a pass." J. J. grins. "I'm dangerous to myself, they think. To others? Probably, they say. A man with my complexity needs a quiet environment. I'm not boarding any transports to your sister's. It's Kingsbridge for me."

"Kingsbridge?"

"VA bin. My place of residence. Except visitors don't find the plastic chairs in the dayroom too comfortable. Trackman, you might not mind the chairs."

He scans the small, serious face, the head nodding at him now, twitching restlessly, the fingers drumming. The man could be Ho Chi Minh's younger brother if he were shorter, stiller. "I like plastic," he says.

J. J. empties his shot glass. "Enough whiskey and our dreams are sweet, even standing up. Think I'll take some fresh air." Suddenly his narrow back is swirling past tables, heading toward the exit.

Well, Papa-san, the only other man in the world who's met you, and he's out on a pass. He drinks until not a drop of beer is left. Then finds his way back to the phone booth, and dials Pauli's number, still wondering where J. J. went.

—Yeah, me again.

—Still here.

—Because my friend is someone I won't see twice.

—What do I want? Like money or something?

—I want to know if you remember the old wedding dress.

—The one hanging in the foyer that you wore on Halloween.

—The party at Patrick's. His father had the guns in the cellar.

—Patrick.

—We used to take my records there.

—Wrong.

—The police came to the storefront.

—Because I called them.

—Because that guy had you pinned to a wall.

—No. They took us home.

—Pa? What difference can it make now?

—One more thing.

—Yes, now. Do you ever think about those years?

—I know they weren't great, but they happened.

—Just a hole?

—Is that where you dropped me?

—Yeah, yeah, I haven't forgotten. I'm getting in the car now.

He scans the tables, but no J. J. His body is heavy, and as ever his head is beating, beating like a bass drum. Papa-san, we can't leave a man in that condition roaming the streets. Besides he needs to tell J. J. where he's going and when and why.

Outside it's getting dark. A neon sign floats purple into the corner of his eye, and turning, he reads, "PO's COZY NOOK." He hears Ida's laugh, gravelly, like a gleeful bark. She'd savor the name the way she savors all oddities. Even him. If she were here, and suddenly he wishes she were, she'd have some questions for J. J. He looks up and down the narrow sidewalk. No man can hold that much liquor and remain standing. "Hey," he whispers. "J. J.?" Across the street, a small park, a few benches, some trees, lots of bushes. He makes his way there, checking from time to time to see if Po's Cozy Nook is still where he left it. His eyes slide over rubbish-filled lawns. "J. J.," he calls a little louder. "I want to say good-bye. I have no time. Understand?"

He steps between benches. Mugger's heaven. No people, no dogs. Just scrambling squirrels. "Hey, J. J.," he yells. "Reveal your fucking self." Some pigeons flutter upward from a waterless fountain.

He rides his hand over dry scratchy bushes, thinking any second J. J.'ll pop up, grinning the way kids do when they startle you at hide-and-seek. That's what he used to call their nighttime rides—hide-and-seek. The man's probably too drunk to move, or maybe he's not J. J. at all. He never did check those tags. Whoever the hell he is, let him collapse in some pissy park. Sleep it off. But what if the man's in trouble? What if, Papa-san?

"J. J.," he shouts. "It's okay, man! Come the fuck on out! I won't leave! I swear it! No more games!"

He veers down another path. Who needs this shit? Parks spook him. Even his daily sprints through Riis Park are not without static. His heart thumps and an iron band wraps itself around his head as he speeds ahead of terror. His heart is doing a very uneven jig. Pills plus beer. Plus J. J. Maybe there never was a J. J. No one here but you and me, Papa-san.

He drops onto a bench. It's darker now. J. J.'s probably curled under some bush. Why not? "Sleep is sleep. Who's going to bother us anymore?" he mutters. "No one. Not here. Not over there." He knows what he needs to do. To be new, he thinks, like a baby is new. To start over. There, not here, except there's no time to grow up again. It's always a trade-off, wouldn't you say, Papa-san?

He breathes in deeply. The old chest hurts. But it's physical, just physical. His arms slide across the splintery wood of the bench as gently as if he were about to stroke Ida's bare shoulders. Once more his body's settling into darkness, but he can't let it. He must finish up. There's the conversation with Pauli that's got to end. That's a beginning, a beginning of an end anyway. Words can't be left floating in the air. He hoists himself to his feet, then one small step at a time crosses the street. No stars, no moon, just the glow of neon to guide him.

The music reaches him as he pushes open the door, so does that smoke. No J. J. He goes straight to the phone this time. Maybe she's ready for bed. It's ringing. Jesus, maybe she's out looking for him. Maybe on her way here, except she doesn't know where here is. He hangs up. Checks the number, the pencil marks a blur. Dials again.

—Hey, Pauli.

—One question.

—Yeah, still here.

—How come you never came down to that goddamn bus station?

—Port Authority, armpit of Manhattan, U.S. of A.

—Why? To pass me the good good-bye in case I didn't return.

—Wait, don't answer. Another thing, how come you never looked for me?

—After I came back. Don't answer.

—You knew where to look. Wait, let me finish.

—Were you afraid because I fought in that goddamn war? Because you didn't want anything to do with a vet, scum of the earth you marched on?

—Don't answer that. Were you afraid I would menace you? Is that what you think? Don't answer that either. Well, who the fuck gave you the right to hate the war more than I did?

His pulse racing, his breath short, he leans his forehead on the cool, metal plate of the phone and waits for the rush of adrenaline to subside. The quiet gathers into a hum in his head. He ought to say something. He wishes she would. He straightens and he scans the area for J. J. He hears Pauli sniffling, or is it static on the line? Shit. He doesn't want to know. He slams the receiver down with a vehemence that scares him.

He searches out the music box, slides the quarters in one at a time, listening as each makes contact with its source. He presses the buttons a bunch of times, then waits for the mellow sounds that will soothe his head. He finds his way back to the phone, too tired now to drive anywhere. And dials Ida.

—Hi, baby.

—Slightly drunk.

—Too far from you right now.

—How'd you guess? Po's Cozy Nook, near the clinic, Two Hundred and Fourth Street.

—How long will you take, baby? I miss you.

—Not that drunk. I have a serious matter to discuss.

—Not on the phone.

—It can't wait more than an hour.

—I made a decision, baby, and it feels so good, almost as good as you.

—No, never got to her. I'm about to phone her again.

—Don't drive too fast, just hurry. I love your voice.

—Yeah, other parts, too.

He dials Pauli.

—Me.

—How'd you like to come down for a beer and some music. My girlfriend Ida'll be here.

—It's easy. Follow the Deegan to Kingsbridge, at the sign turn left onto Two Hundred and Fourth Street, a bar, Po's Cozy Nook. It's right on the corner.

—One more thing.

—Did you do what you wanted?

—The way you spent your time, the way you lived it?

—Over there? I made myself stop thinking about everything here, but when I got home it didn't work the other way around.

—It doesn't matter. I'm going back.

—To the city of Ho, which it wasn't when I left.

—To pick up lost time.

—So they tell me.

His body rocking gently.

—No, just tired.

—I'll be here.

He hangs up, moves back into the barroom, his eyes still searching, but no longer expecting J. J. The room is emptying. Must be later than he thought. People need to sleep to push through. Ida will drive them to a motel.

One of his songs is playing. Sinatra's unchanging voice re-assures him. He wonders if Pauli will actually come. She might. She used to be some good dancer. He closes his eyes, sees them fox-trotting around the tables. The light not too dim, not too bright. The air neither hot nor cold, all extremes in temporary abeyance.

6. AFTER BIG SUR

IDA / SARA-JO / EMMA

■ In the darkness Ida slides out of bed. Begins walking briskly around the room. She mustn't shout. Sara-Jo's asleep. The excitement rising like yeast in an oven. She paces until it's contained. Then turns on the light. She's going with him. It's the only way. He'll have to agree. She'll make him. "Have some tea," she whispers. And tiptoes downstairs.

Sara-Jo, in shorts and halter, sits cross-legged on the pink-flowered couch, a magazine open on her lap.

"Why aren't you sleeping?"

"Why aren't you?" Sara-Jo stares at her.

"I was thirsty."

"I can't sleep."

She considers pouring her an inch of bourbon. Instead drops into the lime-colored chair. "There's a window fan, if it's too hot down here."

"It's not the heat, Ida. Something deeper." Sara-Jo flings the magazine aside.

"Can I do anything for you?"

"Like what?"

"Oh, I don't know. Dance? Sing?"

Sara-Jo smiles.

"Tomorrow won't be so bad. You'll like them. They're the best family around."

"It's just another vet's house."

"Rod's different."

"Yeah, sure. Why can't I stay here with you? You're the only one who doesn't piss me off. Remember when I used to run away and hide in your big closet. Are the toys still in there?"

"Probably. Is that what you're doing? Running away?"

"No. I've got my mother's blessing. You know how I hated California, Ida. The weather leaves people soggy. It took forever for a teacher to finish a sentence."

"You exaggerate. Anyway, you'll like Rod and Emma. They're very sane."

"Oh, give me a break."

"Your mother doesn't want you back in the old high school. I can't blame her. The kids are wild there."

"And the ones in the Bronx are tame? Really? Where do you people come from? Besides, I'm not influenced easily. I do what I want. I don't even like the kids around here, they're so whiny."

"Well, that's a breakthrough." She walks over, takes Sara-Jo's hands, and pulls her to her feet. "Come on, lovey, let's make you a cup of tea with honey. It does a job, you know."

She deposits her on one of the chairs at the kitchen table. First, she'll rent out the house. If she can't, well, she won't worry. There's nearly five thousand in her savings account. If she has to, she'll blow every penny. A nurse can always find a job. That's what she'll tell Frankie. A nurse can always find a job.

She heats water, searches out the honey.

"You have no reason to be so chipper," Sara-Jo says.

"And you're real sweet, too."

"I don't feel sweet."

"Just relax."

"Ida, I can't. It's my personality."

"Then write poems."

"What?"

"Kids like you should write poems instead of griping."

"Don't you want to speak to me tonight?"

"Lovey, I've figured out something that I can't discuss just yet, and my head's full."

She serves Sara-Jo the tea, sits at the table with her, staring at the wall calendar. It's been there for years—always at January—because the white cranes flying toward her from a distant gray sky is her favorite scene.

▪ The dream wakes him. He turns on the bed lamp: 3:30. He eyes the white box of pills. One and he'll be walking on marshmallows. Better to hold still, let the nausea pass. If it ever does. Once he's back to 'Nam, he won't sleep at all. And that's okay too. Right, Papa-san?

His eyes rest on the carton filled with record albums. Ol' Blue Eyes, Bennett, LaRosa. Maybe he'll drop them off at the hospital. The old men'll like them. The old men and him. He'd leave them here, but they're not Rod's kind of music, or Emma's. He's not sure what to leave them. Something great for putting up with him. Like what? His Purple Heart?

"Hey, Papa-San," he whispers, "want to hear some music

from the Chairman of the Board?" He kneels to pull out an album, but they're packed so tightly and the cramps are spreading up his calves. He begins to limp around the room. "Papa-san, how come you're so old and spry, and I'm so young and dry?" he mutters. "Man, this place is just too small."

Quietly descending the stairs to the kitchen, he swipes a Bud from the case beneath the sink. "Papa-san, let us enjoy the rest of this night." He twists off the cap and hobbles through the swinging white door into the living room. Laura is sitting on the floor, talking to a small doll clutched in her hand. It's the third time this week he's found her this way.

"Hey, vixen," he whispers. "What's up?"

"Me," she says.

"You're a real joker," he says as the next wave of nausea rolls the bitterness into his throat. Slowly, slowly he sinks toward the couch. Head back, eyes closed, he tells himself that the airplane's in for a crash landing.

"Frankie?" She clambers up beside him.

He reaches over and musses the thick, curly hair, wondering how long it'll be before she forgets him. He takes a long swallow of the warm beer. Bitterness to bitterness. He opens his eyes. "So, vixen, what're you doing?"

"Waiting for you. Minnie too."

"The two of you been talking?"

"She can't talk. She listens. We heard you in the kitchen."

"How'd you know it was me?" He pushes himself closer to upright.

"Who else could it be?"

Child has got to be older than she looks. "Strange people hang out in normal places, especially in the middle of the night."

"No one'll be able to visit you, my dad says." She's staring at the doll.

"Oh yeah?"

"My dad says there's lots of mosquitoes and you need to be six feet tall to see over the grass. He says, even if you can read it's easy to get lost. He says there are no street signs and you have to carry a compass. And besides, he says the only electricity's in the city and it's hard to find a city, so everyone goes to sleep early. And he says it rains all the time so you have to stay inside dark huts. You won't like it there, Frankie."

"So Rod's been talking up a storm, I guess. But I'm used to all that. I'm tall, and I can see in the dark with my flashlight, and I don't need a compass because I've marked all the paths in my head. But he's right if he says it's not a great place for kids."

"Aren't there any kids there?"

"Lots."

"So?"

"You're giving me a hard time, vixen. I don't know if I can take any more of these questions."

"Momma said not to ask you anything."

"Yeah, she was right. Want to hear about how I met Ho Chi Minh?"

"Who?"

"I was having a smoke, and he came right out of the wood line, with this wispy beard and tight, shiny skin, and eyes so bright they were like negatives held up to a lamp. Sucked me right in. He waves his cane over his head like he knows me, like he's saying hello. Then he lays this rice-paper hand on my cheek. Like magic, it relaxes me. So, what happens, happens. It's all right."

"But who is he?"

"The Santa Claus of Vietnam."

"There's no Santa Claus."

"Yeah, well, there ought to be."

"I don't think so."

"Why not?"

"I don't like waiting all year not to see him on one night."

"What if you didn't see him once a month?"

"Are you ever coming back?"

Leave it to Beaver to ask the question, he thinks.

"Momma says she needs to rent out your room."

"Yeah, well." He finishes another long drink. "How about I carry you back to bed so I can stretch out here."

"I can go by myself."

"You mad at me, vixen."

"She is." Laura points at the doll, as she disappears through the doorway.

Yeah, Papa-san, life will go on. He stuffs the small, hard pillow under his throbbing head.

▪ No one'll stir until she gets out of bed. Except Frankie, who may or may not be there on the couch. Emma's eyes slide to the clock: 6:40, then to the gray light seeping through the slats of the window blinds. She's been awake for at least an hour, her mind racing among possibilities. It's not a good idea, she's sure. They have to discuss it some more.

Rolling away from Rod's body, pressed against her back, she sits up, waits, hears him stir. "I've been thinking about Sara-Jo," she says. "My bones tell me we shouldn't do it."

He stretches. "She's just a kid like ours."

"That's not what I hear."

"You don't know her."

"Neither do you."

"What's to know?" He yawns.

"We didn't bring her up, Rod. Why should she listen to us if her own mother can't manage her?"

"Give it a chance."

"Ida says you can't say Rooster's name to her."

"Poor Rooster," he mumbles.

"The room's easy to rent. It's big, there's all that light."

"That's not the point." He folds his arms under his head. "This is Rooster's kid. I owe him."

"Did he save your life?"

"You know he didn't."

"So?"

"Emma, I've got you, the children, he has nothing."

"Is that your fault?"

"It's not his either."

She sighs. "Laura's missing Frankie something awful and he hasn't even left yet. I hoped maybe we could leave the room open for a week or two, until she forgets a little."

"I'll miss him, too. Besides, I already said yes to Millie on the phone."

"Bastard." She gets out of bed.

"Ida's bringing her around this morning."

"What?"

"She wants her to meet us before she moves in." His words too quick. "I'll take us all out for breakfast."

"With what? The small change in your pockets? Laura's beads?"

"Sure, the pretty blue ones."

"Rod, this isn't a game. It's not fair me having to care for a third child." She scrolls up the blinds. The air's moist and warm.

"I'll help. I always do."

"But you won't worry, you'll leave that to me."

"That's your nature. Besides, she's not a child-child. And our Beth will have someone to go to school with."

"Beth doesn't need anyone else, she has her own friends."

"She can show Sara-Jo the ropes." He swings his legs off the bed.

"More likely the other way."

"Well, our Beth is a little grim for her age."

"Grim? Rod! Where the fuck is your head?"

"Pardon me?"

"Worried. She's worried, not grim."

"What does she have to worry so much about?"

"Maybe having to work after school and maintain her marks."

"All right. Enough. Sara-Jo's my buddy's child. She needs. We can't say no."

"You can't," she mumbles. "Did you tell Millie what the rent will be?"

"Yeah." He stands, pulls on a T-shirt.

With Rod working at least the next three weeks, she thinks, plus her own job, plus Millie's rent money . . . No, she'll never get dressed if she continues figuring. She opens the closet. "Maybe your father'll find you some work again next month." Finds her jeans.

"Yeah."

"If we receive Millie's check on time plus your . . ."

"Not now, Emma. It's too early."

"Okay. At least we won't miss a month's rent on the room."

He turns to face her. "You always manage. You're a wizard. So quit counting."

"Some wizard. I make money out of money, just like the rich." She searches out a short-sleeved blouse.

"Millie's just making ends meet. She says she has a lot of new expenses."

"It's tough with one salary."

"Frankie only had himself to worry about."

A cold fist lodges in her throat, the blouse slips from her hands. "What rent did you charge her?" Her voice a whisper.

"Fifty dollars less."

She drops into the chair.

"Emma, come on."

She stares at his sunburnt arms, dark against his white shirt.

"Stop looking that way. No one died."

"That's the gas and electric money."

"I couldn't say 'Sorry, Millie, take your child elsewhere.' Would you really expect me to do that, turn her down because she's broke? Answer me."

"Why didn't you tell me right away?"

"Because you didn't want Sara-Jo here in the first place."

"When were you planning to let me know?"

"Tomorrow. The next day. I wasn't planning, that's all."

"You've stopped talking things over with me."

"You're blowing this up."

"It's bad if we can't talk."

"Then stop acting like I'm one of the kids and you're the adult. For God's sake, I care about the family, too."

"But you don't care if the electricity's turned off. You just light candles and play ghost games with the girls."

"That's right. So it's turned off. We scrape up the money, pay, and it's turned on again. Then we blow out the candles. Big deal. Do you want the bathroom?"

She doesn't answer.

He moves past her.

She wills back the tears. And if there's no money to turn the lights back on, what then?

She finishes dressing. Walks past Frankie dead out on the couch. Through the kitchen window she sees a sparrow hopping from lawn to chair to swing. She moves automatically from pantry to sink to stove, setting up the coffee pot, boiling water for the oatmeal, pulling cartons of milk and orange juice out of the fridge, trying to remember anything positive she's heard about Sara-Jo, but it's Millie that's on her mind. Millie in California making a new life for herself, while she, here, has to care for her child. Why can't Sara-Jo move into Lucy's apartment? That's what she should've told Millie. She doesn't want someone else to worry about. Damn.

"Mom?"

"Lord, you scared me."

"Why aren't you still in your robe?" Beth asks.

"We've having company any minute, although your father forgot to tell us." The harshness in her tone leaves Beth staring. The child watches her too closely. "That man, he's getting old." She pushes Beth gently toward the stove. "Here, stir, or you'll have lumpy cereal."

"Mom, I saw Ida through the upstairs window." Laura, in pajamas, walks slowly into the room.

"Get dressed, we're having company."

"Ida's not company. And Frankie's still sleeping."

"Do as I say." She turns Laura around. "Go ask Daddy to help you."

"I can dress myself."

She begins to set the table. Then Rod is thumping downstairs, opening the front door, welcoming them. When she looks up, she sees Rooster's blue eyes in a porcelain face. She ought to hug the girl.

"Where's Frankie?" Ida kisses her cheek, dropping the scent of primrose.

"Right here, baby." He has his arm around Laura. "Well, well, whole crowd's arrived. Hey, Sara-Jo. Long time."

"Yeah. I'm going to wash up."

"Laura, show her the bathroom, then get dressed."

"I'll find it."

"Friendly tyke."

"She doesn't like vets," Ida says.

"Can't blame her."

Sara-Jo locks the bathroom door. Sits on the aqua toilet seat, her legs out in front of her. Takes note of the gray tile, the matching floor mat, the sponges along the bath rim, the full-length mirror hinged onto the back of the wooden door. Nothing new here.

She goes to the sink, opens small vials and boxes. The good stuff is always in the bedroom. Emma's diaphragm, no doubt, hidden in some drawer, like her mother's. Maybe she'll find a few free condoms there. But maybe men that old don't wear them. Maybe. Anyway, when she makes some money, she'll get a prescription for the pill. Whenever that'll be.

She reaches into her purse. Takes out what's left of a joint, lights up, inhales, holding the smoke deep inside her chest. Her eyes close. She exhales slowly, sees Carlos's big square face, those soft brown eyes of his. "No problem, the Bronx is around the corner," he'd whispered when she told him the address. Inhaling once more, she flips the roach into the toilet. Presses the lighter back inside her purse. Lets some water trickle over her hands before flushing.

The cereal bowls are white clouds on blue sky. The bread, a long brown arm on a silver bed. She takes her seat, the sweet, acrid taste still on her tongue. No one's eating. Maybe they're waiting for her. Maybe she interrupted grace. She looks around. Emma's pouring coffee into cups. Not hers. They think she's a kid. Like their kids. They see what they want. No mind. She's tired of letting people know how to treat her. She picks up her spoon, looks into the rising smoke of the coffee.

"Frankie can show you the room. You can fix it up your own way." The first words she's said to the girl. And they hardly make it through her tight lips.

Sara-Jo shrugs. "It'll be a room like any other. I've been there."

"Where's Laura," her voice loud.

"You sent her to get dressed, Mom." Beth looks at her strangely.

"I bet you miss California," Rod says.

"What's to miss." Sara-Jo begins to eat.

"People must get tired of all that sun."

She wishes they'd stop talking to her. "I didn't notice."

"I nearly forgot." Ida holds up a jar of greenish liquid. "For Frankie."

"Emma'd never serve up anything like that, would you?" Rod reaches for her hand. She pulls away.

"Joke all you want," Ida says, "this stuff is healthy."

"I'm not drinking it," Frankie insists.

"It cures tiredness."

He shakes his head.

Emma grabs the jar, pours the liquid into a glass, sets it down in front of him. "Go on, you've had worse."

Frankie moves the glass to Rod.

"I won't drink anything that color."

"I thought you guys drank everything," Sara-Jo says.

Rod looks at her. "Did you really?"

Frankie stares at Ida. "What's in this, anyway?"

"Seaweed."

"What're you doing to my ol' buddy." Rod leans over, pats Frankie on the back.

"Lots of people eat seaweed," Sara-Jo says.

"Who?" Beth demands.

"People in other lands just as good as we are." Sara-Jo's staring at Rod.

"Well, what do you know." He returns the gaze. "We've got a little hippie here."

"Those were your times, not mine."

"You're spunky. That'll get you places."

"Damn straight it will."

"That and a quarter," says Frankie.

"Sara-Jo, what point are you making?" Ida asks mildly.

"No point. No point at all."

"So tell me, is seaweed always green?" Frankie asks.

"Honey, just drink it, it's good."

"Just toss it out." Sara-Jo reaches for the glass.

"Hey, that's mine." Frankie drinks it down. "I'm filling with energy," he whispers to Sara-Jo.

She refuses to respond.

"Look," Beth points.

Laura, still in pajamas, stands in the doorway, her mouth a red slash, her cheeks rouged, gold earrings clipped to her ears.

"Who are you?" Rod asks.

"An adult."

"That's it." Emma gets up and grabs Laura by the arm.

"Where we going?"

"To wash off that junk."

"Ida wears it."

"Shut up."

"Loving family," Sara-Jo mutters, flashing Ida some raised eyebrows.

▪ Ida watches for Frankie from the second-floor window. The streetlamps are on, and across the wide avenue she can just see the entrance to the Bronx Zoo. Except for the occasional rumble of a passing truck, it's quiet.

The room is small, neat, square, the bedspread beige, the headboard beige, the walls a creamy pink. None of it the least bit cheery, but it's a place to be without the others and no matter what he says, it's easier for him not to drive out to her house. That's what she wants to do, make everything easy. It's why she lifted the mat of lamb's wool from the hospital. So he could take it with him. The heat there will dry out his skin even more. She'll pack it, make sure he sleeps on it. She squirms into the tan chair of make-believe leather, anxious for him to arrive, nervous about telling him. A drink would help, but she'll wait for him. The Jack Daniel's in her bag, the Styrofoam bucket filled with ice, and she's already set the glasses on the dresser. She can see them twice, once in the mirror. It's bad luck to drink alone. Deede sneers at her superstitions. Insists on walking under ladders, putting keys on tables. Deede's face still haunts her. Tearless, grim, strangely defiant. She wouldn't let anyone near her at Jason's funeral. Only Kevin, Tess, and Aristotle were allowed in the first pew. She can't bear being kept from Jason's son this way.

"Frankie, where are you?" She says it aloud, and goes again to the window that overlooks the parking area. Only twenty minutes late. That's not unusual. Still, she's been waiting all day to share her decision. The white Toyota takes a sharp turn into the lot, pulling quickly into a space. She hears the music stop abruptly, the lights go off. And joy rises inside her. He sees her, calls up, "Dangerous neighborhood."

"Ssh," her finger to her lips.

"A bear walked right down Southern Boulevard."

Sliding away, she wonders how many he's had. She unrolls the cylinder of lamb's wool onto the bed. Hurries to make the two drinks, greets him at the door, the glass in her hand. He kisses her lips, takes the drink.

"Isn't this a little extravagant?" He looks around.

"Extravagant would have room service." She pushes him gently into the chair, sits on its arm, removes his cap, feels the fuzz of new hair. Remembers the funny potato plant that sprouted grass when placed in water. "It's coming back."

"Just like you said, once the treatments ended."

"They didn't end, Frankie, you stopped them."

"Baby, who wants to spend a short life waiting in clinics? Besides, I'm into alternatives. I drink seaweed and I believe in the ancient art of healing."

"And what's that?"

"The laying on of your hands." He runs a finger along the outside of her strong thigh, feels her muscles tense.

She slips off the chair arm. They need to talk first. "Okay, I'll give you hands," she says, dragging the lamb's wool onto the floor. "Belly down. I'll massage your back."

"What's this?"

"Magic carpet." Tell him now, she thinks, and kneels, watching him slowly unbutton his shirt, remembering the once-heavy shoulders, the thick braids of muscles in his forearms. Skin that coppered easily now kept hidden from the sun lest it dry and crack and be sore even to the softest touch. At work, her patients are members of other people's families. She dutifully charts their losses: "Less appetite." "Less output." "Less energy." How else to remember? With Frankie she can't forget. She rubs the nap of the lamb's wool in which she'd like to safely wrap him. "Shit, Frankie."

He, too, kneels. He takes her hands.

"Shit," she repeats.

"Yeah, baby, friend, lover, jewel, all there in that wonderful body of yours that I can't even fuck properly."

"Ssh, stop. I'm sorry, I planned to be upbeat."

"It's the truth."

She makes herself smile.

He sees nothing gay in her eyes. "I don't make you laugh anymore, do I?"

"You? A sense of humor? Since when?" She kisses his lips. "I don't feel like laughing. I don't even want to." She takes the moisture cream from her bag, tips the pink lotion into the cup of her palm. Tell him now.

He lies, his face on crossed arms, the soft, furry rug under his belly. "I stopped taking the damn night pills and now my dreams have music. Has that ever happened to you?"

"I don't think so." She smoothes the lotion across his back. If it were her body, she'd take the treatments, swallow the pills, follow each directive, fight for every minute more it bought her. Yet a few hours of music in his head makes him happy. God, it's why she loves him, isn't it? She slides the lotion down toward his waist, up onto his shoulder blades, along the sides of his neck.

The cool, minty smell reminds him of the VA hospital, the supply closet where some of the guys and he would hole up to have a few drinks before each infusion. "Great, baby."

Now, she thinks. Now. Her palm flat on his vertebrae. "I'm going with you."

He rolls over, props himself on his elbows.

"I'm coming with you."

"You can't."

"I can."

"What do you plan to do there? Visit the mall? Take a walk in the mud. Don't go nuts on me. Please. Not now. Rub a little more of that magic into my skin." He rolls back over.

"I'll volunteer at one of the hospitals. A nurse can always get a job. I've thought it all out." She wipes her wet palms.

"No."

"You can show me that moon, honey, the one that hangs between those mountains so orange it breaks your eyeballs. Remember? Frankie, I don't want to be here as long as you're somewhere else that I can be, too. Don't you want me with you?"

"Not there. It's dangerous." He sits up, facing her.

"The war's over, Frankie. People go there on vacation."

"Not me."

"I know."

"Good. End of discussion."

"Don't get angry at me. I love you."

"It's only time. I'll be back."

He won't. She knows it. He knows it. You don't return from there twice. "Consider the idea."

"I have. It's wrong. I don't want you there alone, having to deal with any shit that might happen to me. I don't want a nurse." He gets up, pours himself a refill.

"A nurse? Is that who I am?"

"That's what you'll end up being. A nurse. My nurse. It's not the way I see it."

"How do you see it?"

"Beautiful good-byes. No blood. No gore. Mainly no pus. It's what I want. Okay? It's what I need." His eyes burn into hers.

"What about what *I* want? You make me know how wonderful I am. I can't know it by myself. I can't know it alone. It'll all go away with you. I don't want you noble. Just us to last a little longer. I don't care where."

"Listen, you won't fall apart." His voice rough, the veins in his slim neck stretched taut. "I know all about you. You move boulders to get where you need to be. You're strong. I don't *ever* have to worry about you. That's the only peace I have. Don't take that away from me, understand?" His body so wired now, it could shatter into a million fragments.

"Okay," she whispers quickly. "Okay." And slides into the chair, which he begins circling.

"I have a story for you, baby. It's about this vet in Santa Fe. He really exists. Every few days, no matter where he is, he screams until he loses his voice. Then when his voice heals he does it all over again. He scares me more than going back."

She nods.

"Besides, Papa-san's pining, he wants to go home. No more wandering, see?"

She nods again.

"You'll be there with me, understand? Rod, too. Just the way Papa-san is. Get it? I'm not nuts, baby. I just take stuff with me, whatever I need. It happens when I travel long distances." He shakes his head, trying to rid it of the crowding, the buzz, the hissing, and leans against the wall.

His face is a white mask. She moves toward his body, a body held together by sheer will, the will to complete a circle she's not part of. She tugs him into bed, one hand propping up the pillows behind him. Then climbs in too. Shoulder to shoulder.

"Say it," he whispers.

"What?"

"Why I'm returning."

"To get clean."

"I love your lips."

"And the rest of me."

"All of you. Just like Ol' Blue Eyes sings."

▪ The cascading waters are quiet now, the green lights beneath turned off. A man retreats ahead of the wide, soapy arcs of his mop. Sara-Jo sits on the rim of the fountain and gazes around the empty mall. One after another, the lit-up faces of the dark stores climb the spiraling tiers like a roller coaster without sound. "Hurry, Carlos," she whispers to the stained-glass window of the restaurant where he works.

They'll go to Jones Beach. She'll lie with his arms around her and breathe in the warm smell of his body.

When he comes toward her in khakis and a white, short-sleeved shirt, she jumps up. They walk quickly into the thick, hot air of the parking lot, the haze a gray belly under the dark sky, and climb into his red Jeep.

With his hands on the steering wheel, he stretches way back. "I hate cleaning other people's messes. You know? It makes my stomach sick."

"You'll find something else."

"What?"

She strokes his tense arm. "Let's go to the beach."

"Cuckoo kid. The beach? Everyone's there tonight. It's hot."

He has a point.

"Where's Ida?"

"With Frankie."

"So, Sara-Jo?" He ruffles the back of her hair, sticks the key in the ignition.

On Sunrise Highway, the hot air turns cool around her neck and arms. They glance at each other.

"If Ida's not home in an hour, the place is ours. Anyhow, it's my last night there."

He drops her a quick hug. "I told you, the Bronx is a half-hour by Jeep. No sweat. Okay? Smile for me, make me happy. It's been a strange day."

"I spent the morning at my new digs."

"So?"

"What I expected."

"A mean man? Bad woman? Crazy children? Explain."

"Not worth it."

"Play the Sting tape."

"Natalie Merchant." She retrieves it from the neat stack inside the neat glove compartment, presses it into the tape deck. Notices his strong fingers gripping the steering wheel.

"No one's seen you since you returned," he says. "People asking for you."

"Only you wrote me. I've outgrown them."

"Big traveler."

"Don't give me that, you don't play with them either."

"Me? I'm out of there."

"Well, so am I. Tell them that."

"Why should I deliver your messages?"

"So why give me theirs?"

"You sound like a lawyer."

"Maybe that's what I'll be and you can all hire me to get you out of jail." She laughs. The wind blows into her mouth. They're doing eighty on the nearly empty road and she hopes so much Ida won't return home tonight.

When they pull into the street, Ida's car isn't there. It's nearly midnight. Hugging each other's waists, they walk across the small front lawn.

She takes a beer out of the fridge, hands it to him, flips on the air conditioner. The soft whirring divides them from the outside.

He straddles a kitchen chair, stretches his arm across the table. She slips her hand into his.

"You never did say why you came back?" His beagle-sad eyes on her.

She shrugs.

"Did you fight with Millie?"

She shakes her head. "I miss her. I wish she'd visit, but she won't. Maybe if I was sick. Even then I'd have to be very sick."

"My little orphan."

She stares at him. "Look, I'm no baby. I'm on my own and about to make something of it."

"I bet you are. Only who's going to pay?"

"Me. I'll go to school, work, whatever I have to. I'm not about to get stuck, see."

"Why didn't you do it there?"

Her eyes slide past him to the wintry birds on Ida's calendar. She can't explain, hardly understands herself. The sadness that made energy disappear until it was a chore to talk. It scared her mother. It scared her. "Too hot there."

"Yeah, it's real cold here."

She smiles. "New York in my blood."

He gets up, stands behind her, clasps her shoulders, his thumbs making circles on her skin.

She reaches up, pulls his hands tight around her neck. "Where were you this morning? I phoned."

"Visiting the army, navy, marines."

Her body stiffens.

"The navy will fix my teeth for nothing. The marines offer out-training. Ever hear the word? It means a job after."

She stands. "Sure. Just like they gave my father. Collecting fleas on the Lower East Side."

"Baby, that was long ago. This volunteer army wants me. I get to pick and choose. It's a supermarket."

"Do you really believe that?"

"I sign a contract stating what I need. They get my hours."

"Carlos, I don't want to hear it."

"There's no war. It's a cool time to join."

"And if one breaks out?"

"I'll go with the probabilities. It's all I can do."

"They'll teach you to kill."

"I learned that on the street."

She takes another beer out of the fridge. "Are you making this up? It's a joke, right?" She walks behind him, drapes one arm over his shoulder, rests her cheek against his back.

"The only jokes I tell are the ones that make you laugh."

"You can't join now," she whispers, "we've only made love twice. You don't start something like that, then leave."

"After a few weeks, we can be together again."

She drifts slowly toward the window.

"If I stay around here, what's it going to get me?"

In it, she catches her reflection—and his.

"I salute some hillbilly punk from Mountainville, Tennessee, and sleep on a cot. It's better than jail, worse than home, but I'll get something I can use later."

She sets the beer on the table. She's no longer looking at him or his reflection.

"You're not hearing me."

"You'll become one of them." She says it more to herself. "Even if you hate every minute."

"Just because your old man's a crazy vet has nothing to do with me. I'll get out equipped for a better life. Equipped. Not crazy." He sits. "Come here."

"I'm not loving a damn marine."

"Baby, stop it. Why are you hurting me like this? We're so good together."

"If you go away, that's it. I swear, Carlos."

"Shit, Sara-Jo. Doesn't it bother you that I have to dust chairs and vacuum tablecloths? Tell me that's okay?"

"Save money, get into school."

"Hah. I can't even make enough to support my Jeep." He comes over, tries to pry her hands loose from the chair. "Let's talk in bed."

"That's not what we do there."

"You like what we do there?"

She says nothing.

"Don't clam up on me."

She stares past his head at the crooked blue lamp shade. Without him, she'll be lonely in the Bronx.

"Talk to me. I love you, baby."

She allows her gaze to slide back to his sad brown eyes. He kisses her nose, her chin, her mouth. She doesn't kiss him back. He pulls her so close she can see nothing but his chest. He has to take her seriously, she thinks, too comfortable against the warmth of him to say so now.

"Upstairs?" he whispers, still holding her.

They begin their slow climb, passing photos of Ida and Jason, Jason and Frankie, her mother and Rooster, all the bearded men encircling a keg of beer that New Year's Eve she remembers because her mother cried at midnight.

He deposits her on the single bed in the guest room, and sits on the edge. "Are you thinking-quiet or mad-quiet?" He takes off his shoes, his shirt, his pants, lies down naked, his erect penis pressing the dress against her thigh. He strokes her face. "So lovely," he croons, "so lovely."

"Never mention this stuff again," she whispers. "Okay?"

He lifts her hair, nuzzles her neck. "You'll be fine. It'll be fine for us."

"Carlos, listen, say 'I promise I won't join up.' Okay? Promise me that, because I need that promise."

"I can't, baby."

She rolls away. "Why not?"

"I already signed up. This afternoon. You'll get used to it. Don't freak on me, baby, okay? You'll get used to it. I'm scared, too."

She slides off the bed, runs down the stairs, grabs her keys off the table, slams the door behind her. She needs to be somewhere else until he leaves. The first pain is the worst pain, she repeats silently, looking for some shelter. She sees Deede's house down the block and walks there. No lights. They're probably asleep. She sits under the big maple tree on the front lawn, her bare shoulders against the prickly trunk, her ankles crossed on the moist grass. He's wrong. She'll never get used to it. She doesn't want to. Won't let herself.

▪ In the driveway, Ida turns off the ignition. The air inside still cool. This morning his hands were so warm she feared he had a fever, but didn't say so, didn't say anything, really. Just lay there, her head back against his shoulder until the dim light of dawn crept into the room.

Pinching the bridge of her nose, she closes her eyes. This will never do. A kind word from a passing neighbor and she'll dissolve. Slipping the keys into her pocket, she gets out of the car. A thin breeze passing. The narrow street still quiet. She just doesn't know. Without him here, after so many years. Some things are easier to survive than others. She slings the bag over her shoulder. The front door's ajar. It's not like Sara-Jo to be sloppy.

In the kitchen, two nearly full bottles of beer on the table. She walks into the living room. The couch untouched. Sucks in her breath. "Sara-Jo?" she calls, going up to the guest room. "Sara-Jo?" Louder this time. Opens the door. "Sara-Jo?" Crosses the hallway. Taps on the bathroom door. Pushes it open. Sees her lying naked in the tub, only a few inches of water around her. "God." The word low in her throat.

She pushes aside a whiskey bottle, puts one foot in the water, braces herself, and grabs Sara-Jo's shoulders. Sees her breathing. Smells the booze. "Drunk, for God's sake." Shakes her. "Shit." Shakes her again. Sara-Jo's hand flies up. Her eyes open.

"Stop, Ida, stop."

"I'm getting you out of here." But suddenly there's no strength in her, the water dragging at her dress. She sees the red marks of her fingers on Sara-Jo's shoulders. "What happened?"

"Just wanted to sleep for a while. That's all." Sara-Jo hoists herself out of the tub. Pads into the bedroom, grabs a long T-shirt.

She follows. "I thought you were dead." And drops her wet clothing on the floor, wrapping herself in a kimono.

"And if I were? You'd just be pissed." Sara-Jo dangles her legs off the bed. The shirt clings damply to her thin shoulders, her small breasts.

"You scared me." The anger's still in her.

"I planned to have a few drinks, then sleep in the guest room. I didn't expect to pass out in the tub."

"Why the drinks?"

"Carlos joined the marines. He told me last night." The tiny hoops in her ears tremble. "He was going to be my stable moment. What a crock."

Then why isn't Sara-Jo wailing, crying?

"He was going to visit me in the Bronx, but how could he? He'd be gone. He lied." Sara-Jo stares at her.

"He's not going forever." Her tone harsh. Ashamed, she takes a deep breath.

"What's the matter with you? With all of you? Those vets have ruined your lives. Do you think I'd ever let myself in for that?"

Sara-Jo's voice cuts through her. She walks to the dresser, lines up the brush, comb, three bottles of perfume, the hand cream. A row of things less meaningful without Frankie. She looks in the mirror. Who does she see? A woman with good times behind her. So what's wrong with that? She hasn't been unhappy, just lonely now and then. And no more so than women with husbands and children. You see, Sara-Jo, Frankie and I. No, keep him out of it. You see, Sara-Jo, your mother and Rooster were this item. So what did that mean? Sara-Jo will ask and she can't say, except that it was the promise of something more, and God knows they all wanted that. She turns. Sara-Jo has a pillow across her lap. Her elbows resting there.

"I'm not going to explain any of the men to you."

"You don't have to. I already know my father's crazy."

"Maybe he is. Jesus, he was beautiful."

"So I heard."

"Like sweet pears and fire."

"Big deal." Sara-Jo props up the pillow behind her, leans back. "You never had to live with him. I did."

"You're hard, sometimes." She stares at Sara-Jo's smooth, pale forehead, the sweet lift of her sharp chin.

"Because I know what I don't want."

"Because you think you can control everything, even whiskey."

"Don't worry, I hate the stuff. All I wanted was some fast sleep. I knew I'd feel better afterward."

"Do you?" She picks up her dress, drapes it over the chair. Sits there.

Sara-Jo shrugs. "Some."

"So what's your plan with Carlos?"

"I'll never see him again."

"Never?"

Sara-Jo shakes her head slowly, her thin lips pressed together.

Perhaps Sara-Jo knows something about getting past the painful holes that she herself has never learned. "Do you love Carlos?"

"Some. It hasn't been that long."

"If it had been, if you'd known him for years, say?"

"Oh Ida." She laughs. "How can I imagine that? I'm only sixteen."

She nods. "Of course." She's seen women torn away from their men. Some fall apart. Some mend. In time. She wonders how long. "Maybe I'll sleep for an hour. There's a farewell dinner tonight for Frankie."

"When's he leaving?"

"A few days. I planned to go with him." Her words deliberate. "He wouldn't have it. He wants to spare me."

"You'd go there?"

"Why not?"

"Drop everything? Like you had no life of your own?"

"He's part of my life."

"But you have a job. You have friends. You have me." Sara-Jo's glaring at her.

She shrugs. "I have love, my sweets."

"And I haven't?" Sara-Jo swings her legs off the bed.

"Not yet."

"You're wrong."

"About what?"

"About when I do."

"Oh?"

"It won't be blind like yours." They stare at each other. Then Sara-Jo frowns at her. "Can't you just let him go?"

The words hang in the air. She reads them anew. It's what he wants, too. Her eyes slide to the painting from Thailand he sent her years ago. The soft, brown mountains seem to move like sand in a breeze.

"I could try," she says.

"I'll keep you company."

"I'm beginning to think you should go back to your mother."

"No." Sara-Jo jumps off the bed, begins pacing. "I can't be there. She wants so little. It depresses me. All she talked about was seeing Big Sur. How beautiful it would be, how nothing could compare, how going there would be the most exciting experience of her life. If she was right, there'd be nothing left to look forward to."

"You underestimate your mom. She knows more than you imagine. She knows that things would go on, even after Big Sur. They always do, good and bad."

She watches Sara-Jo fit herself into her favorite space on the windowsill. Outside the sky's bluer than the cornflowers on the bedspread. By noon, the sun will whiten all the shadowy walls. By evening, she'll have made it through another day.

▪ Emma leaves the unfolded laundry piled high in the red rubber bucket and goes to sit near the window. Except to complain about the noise the washing machine was making, Rod hasn't spoken to her all evening, just paced around. When does he expect her to do the wash? Shit. She's worn out, too. Hopefully, he'll fall asleep on the couch. Then she can slide into bed. Otherwise, she'll have to wait. She remembers, once, a long time ago, staying with him when he was restless like now. Every few minutes he'd grab onto her as if he needed to keep himself from falling. The next day they were both embarrassed by the bruises.

She glances at the paper folded on the windowsill. The lamplight isn't bright and her eyes are tired and she can't bear to take in anyone else's news just now.

"Well, well, well, look who's brooding." Rod stands in the doorway, his body clad only in shorts, the curly hair on his chest beginning to lighten.

"Did you have a snooze?" she asks.

"Did you have a snooze?" he mocks.

"What is it?"

"I bet you're real happy now." His jaw tight, his blue eyes white with anger.

"What, Rod, tell me."

"One-two-three-a-leary. / You got rid of little Mary."

He must be drunk, his voice so loud. What if the girls hear. She says nothing.

"Pretty nubile Sara-Jo. All gone. Right? Emma waves her little wand. Girl disappears. Oh yeah. Room's empty. Good work."

"I had nothing to do with it."

"It was just magic, you and Ida arriving at the same conclusion."

"Keeping Sara-Jo was Ida's decision. The girl will be company for her."

"Yeah, sure. They can pray together. Tell me, have you already found someone to fill the room, someone who'll pay fifty, seventy-five more?" He sprawls on the bed.

"You're calling me a liar?"

"Worse."

She shuts the door. "Worse?"

"Yes." He pulls the pillows toward him, his voice muffled now. "All you care about is money, money, always money. What about Rooster?"

"What does he have to do with anything?"

"She's his daughter. You threw her out."

Is it happening to her family now? Dear God. *"Ida needs Sara-Jo."* She says each word slowly, as if to a child. As if she couldn't bear to let them go. "With Frankie gone. Understand? *I had nothing to do with it.*" She sits motionless, listening to her suddenly beating heart in the heavy silence of the house. With Frankie gone, there'll be no more padding about in the middle of the night. She'll have to get used to that. "I didn't know having Sara-Jo here meant so much to you," she says hesitantly, her voice softening a bit.

"Must have been a big secret."

"Rod, you're not hearing me." Her voice a whisper now.

"Why listen? Your words have nothing to do with your actions." He stares at her, his arms crossed, the lines in his still-boyish face deeper than she remembers. His eyes hate her, but she has to keep watch on him anyway lest he spin off into space, into some place where she'll never reach him again.

"When Ida phoned this morning, I didn't think it was something I had to discuss with you right away. There was nothing to be done. She had already done it."

"No, it was you who did it." The words smack into her. He looks past her so deliberately that she, too, turns. But out the small square window is only the darkness. Ida did make her wish come true, but could that really be *her* fault?

"I'm not letting any stranger into that room, get it?"

"Okay. We'll keep it open for a while." A warm breeze drifts in, bringing the dank smell of wet earth. The sprinkler's been on all day.

"Not a while. Forever."

"I'm not going to argue with you now."

"*Now!* Don't wait. Say it all." He jumps off the bed. "I'm not going to be handled. See?" His arms go up on either side of the door frame, barring her exit though she hasn't moved a muscle.

"All right. I'll find some more typing to do."

"Oh no. Don't give me that I'll-work-all-night-to-bring-in-five-extra-pennies."

"Fine."

"Stop humoring me!" he shouts.

"You'll wake the girls." The words calm, unlike her heart.

"So they hear us fighting? No one's died. No one will."

"I can't talk to you this way. I won't."

"Poor Emma. Married to a bully she leads around like a circus animal."

"I don't lead you around."

"You just set everything up ahead of time. Keep me in the dark. Protect me from myself. Keep everything under control, including me." He shoots the words at her. His body stretched tight across the doorway.

Her eyes slide to the bed, the top sheet twisted, pillows scattered. Why is this happening? Maybe they're having some kind of mutual seizure and if she can stop her heart from pounding he'll calm down too. No, she decides, they're attached, a long cord pulling too tightly, and she's got to loosen it so they can both breathe.

She stands up. "Let's go to sleep."

"Will everything be better in the morning?"

"Maybe."

"It won't! It'll be exactly the same!"

"Take a Valium, damn it." She needs to lie down, to be still.

He strides toward her, jaw clenched, finger pointing. Rat-a-tat-tat. "Drugs, you want to end it with drugs?"

She grabs his wrist. "I can't fight more. I just can't. I can't breathe, I can't hear, my heart's pounding. It has to wait." Her words quick and pleading.

His face registers pain, nausea, the surprise of an interrupted orgasm, but he doesn't pull away. She lets go of his wrist, amazed because the palpitations have stopped.

He lumbers around the room, picking up the pillows, then rolls on top of the twisted sheet, his back to her. "Go to bed," he mumbles.

The weary tone alerts her. She takes off her robe, edges near him, afraid to touch. Hours seem to pass, though it may be minutes or seconds. She can't tell. She can only tell that he's still awake, eyes probably wide open, staring at the wall. She forces herself out of bed. She slides slowly down the wall to the floor, staring at his face. "They've gone, the palpitations. They happen sometimes."

"Better see a doctor," he recites dully.

"You're not wearing your earring."

"I know." He turns again, leaving her staring at his back. Whatever's wrong with him, she can't fix it tonight.

"Okay, I'll go sleep on the couch," she says, but continues to sit there, waiting for him to stop her or tell her he'll go.

He's buried his face in the pillow, and she knows she can't sit here naked on the floor for long. No telling when one of the girls will come in. Hoisting herself up, she takes her robe from the chair. Leaning over him, she finds the pillow wet. She drops onto the bed beside him, suddenly everything clear to her. How could she not have known? Jason dead. Nick dying. Sean wandering. Rooster not long for this world. And now, Frankie.

She slides her arm around his waist, whispering, "I know, baby, I know."

"I gave him the earring you bought me." His voice hoarse, far away.

"It'll be an amulet."

"He's not coming back."

She moves her belly against the small of his back.

"He was my closest friend."

"Don't say *was*. Not yet. Please."

"I'll take the couch."

"Don't leave me alone."

When he turns, she buries her face in the softness between his neck and his shoulder. "It's Frankie's room. It's there waiting for him, no more boarders."

She looks up. His eyes are no longer angry.

"The thought of him there alone, without us, without anyone," he says quietly.

"It's what he wants."

"How can he be sure? It might be a mistake."

"Not this time."

"You think so?"

"Somehow I do. Ida says he's closing some circle. I believe her."

They're whispering back and forth, something they've done ever since Beth was old enough to understand. "We always whisper in this room," she whispers, smiling for the first time in days.

He kisses her nose, her chin, slides down, begins nuzzling her breasts, his prick hardening, her fingers playing inside his curly hair. Her eyes search out the clock, but the angle of light is wrong, his mouth moving down her stomach, to her navel, to the strip of belly beneath, when she hears running feet. "Shit." And leaps for her robe.

Laura pushes open the door.

"Mommy, I hear Frankie."

Rod, already wrapped in the sheet, rubs his face, swings his legs off the bed. "Honey, it's your imagination."

"No, Daddy, he's walking in his room, back and forth, back and forth. I thinks he wants us."

"Let's go see." Rod stands, the sheet trailing.

"You, too, Mommy."

She takes Laura's hand and they follow Rod down the hallway. The door to Frankie's room is closed. She can't remember why. Rod pushes it open, turns on the lamp. The bed is made. On the dresser some empty pill bottles and several packages wrapped in newspaper. The windows are wide open.

"You heard something outside," Rod says.

Laura squeezes her hand, her whole body quiet. She watches intently as Rod checks out the closet, then kneels to look under the bed.

"Daddy, why are you doing that? Frankie wouldn't be under the bed. He's no monster."

She's about to smile when she catches the look on Laura's stricken face. "Listen, sweetpie, we all miss him."

"Then send Daddy out to find him, and bring him back."

"It's too far. Even Daddy can't go there."

"Then we'll never see him again?" Laura stares at them accusingly.

Rod turns away.

"I don't think so," she whispers, frightened because she can't protect her child. Even words of consolation have deserted her. All that's left is the truth.

▪ The guest room, Sara-Jo's now, is bare except for a bed, a rocking chair. That suits her. Ida probably expects her to fix it up in a neon way. Wrong. No rock stars hanging over her head. But she'll sand down the damn door so it'll close and lock properly. How else to have a joint now and then, a few tokes before eye-closing time. To everyone, their relaxation. Good dope, real privacy, and she'll get by.

If she can make enough money to pay for some food and part of the telephone bill, she won't be a total dependent. She's already yellow-lined some part-time jobs: a mother's helper, two coffeehouses, one mall restaurant. Carlos will be gone, but the mall's not her first choice.

Ida's place isn't her first choice either. It's the best of the worst. With Frankie gone, at least the vets won't be hanging around. The way Ida acts with them. Ugh! So soapy sweet, so accepting. Just like her mother. May the force save her from ever losing her personality to a man. At least they've taught her what not to do.

Flinging out her arms, she whirls across the room. Then, lifting a leg onto the bed, she stretches her calf muscles.

No, it won't be long now. She'll get her own place, no roommates, no parents, not even a dog. Just her and loud music whenever she wants. If she decides to stay awake all night, so be it. Freedom is not being watched. She'll get there. She's already on her way.

LUCY

■ "Lucy, it's me, from a pay phone. I have a favor to ask."

"The answer's no."

"This is serious."

"You're always serious, Ida."

"Sean needs a place to stay."

"Tess's Sean?"

"Not anymore."

"The answer's no. No joking."

"It's only for a week."

"That bum walked out on his family."

"He sees his daughter."

"Big deal. He can't stay here. I'm a woman alone."

"You have an extra bedroom, and you're not a teenager."

"Damn right. I survived that and I don't have to share anymore. Besides, I'm not lonely."

"I'm not fixing you up, for God's sake."

"That's what they all say."

"You're being impossible."

"I can't have Sean living here."

"For a week? It's not exactly the rest of your life."

"Besides, the extra bedroom's for the children when they visit."

"And you expect either of them in the next week?"

"No. But if Sean doesn't leave after one week, I'll shoot him. Or you."

"I believe it."

"Good."

▪ Lucy rubs her toes into the white pile of the carpet. Through the window the sun begins to color the treetops. In her fantasy, this is the country, not Central Park. And below, beyond her sight, the fields stretch out for miles. They, too, will soon be anointed with light.

Breaking off a piece of bagel, dipping it into the coffee, she hopes Sean will sleep until she leaves. All the years of getting up earlier than the children have wedded her to this time, solitary, short-lived, before the tumult. It's still difficult to believe that part's over. The house sold at a profit. No more long hours at the beauty salon. Her new job at the nursing home is nine to five. She doesn't miss any of the past, not at all.

"Pretty day coming." He fills the doorway in jeans. Soiled, worn, and cheap-looking.

She says nothing.

He empties the pot of coffee, then points to her wild, frizzy hair. "How do you do that?"

"It's too early for small talk."

He drops into the green chair, interrupting her view of the park.

"Some apartment."

"I like it." She takes a sip of coffee, feels the bagel crumbs like grit on her tongue.

"Must cost you a pretty penny, huh?"

"It's still far from Fifth Avenue, you know." The memory of the neighborhoods she traipsed through to find something safe and affordable makes her glad all over again to be settled here.

"Well." He stretches. "Someday I'll find the right kind of job and start saving."

Fat chance. He's a floater, like his friends.

He opens the balcony door, letting out the air conditioning. The air's humid, the New York soot waits to ride her carpet. "Could you shut that?"

With a small kick, he obliges, then turns to her. "There's something I need to do today."

Curiosity invites trouble. She knows these men come at things sideways to lessen their impact. That's one thing her sister Millie taught her. She goes into the kitchen to make another pot of coffee. She ought to take a week off and visit Millie. She's never been to California, never been anywhere really.

Across the counter that partially divides the two rooms, she notes him leaning against her freshly painted wall. If she hadn't let him stay here, he'd be out on the streets like her brother-in-law. Poor Rooster. Millie says he's doing just what he wants, but she'll never believe it. She parts the lips of the shiny, white coffee bag, takes in the opulent aroma of hazelnut, recalling with satisfaction its expense. It's okay to offer him another cup now that she can afford to buy more.

He's up on the stool, his empty mug on the counter. She dumps four heaping teaspoons into the waiting filter, presses

the button, listens to the steady drip of the water, to the muffled sounds of traffic twelve floors below. In the hallway,
someone slams a door. Sean's eyes are Irish blue, his jaw
stronger than she wants it to be. He looks younger than his
years. Her eyes slide to his broad shoulders. A healthy man.
Unlike her husband, Nick, wasting away with ALS, a disease
with a name so complicated that no one speaks it aloud. Every
time she sees him he seems smaller, weaker. Every time the
same story, the same beginning, middle, and end. And she just
lets him go on. But what else can she do? Something, anything, dear God, to end the endlessness of it. The family goes
less often. She can't blame them. Nick doesn't either. He's too
tired to blame anyone.

Sean's hand waves across her face.

"Blink, lady."

She pours them each another cup of coffee. It's dangerous
to dwell on Nick. He's told her not to a thousand times. She
sighs.

"Those incredible eyes of yours didn't blink for so long I
thought you'd left me."

"I'm not with you."

"It's just an expression." His voice takes on an edge. So
what. She places a carton of milk on the counter. But they
each take it black. He's making her nervous. She hasn't had a
man around for years. Doesn't even remember the difference
between flirting and sarcasm. Maybe there isn't any. Incredible eyes. She watches him take his mug into the living room.
"Please use a coaster." She tosses him one. He makes a show
of placing it on the wooden table, shuffling it this way and
that, before setting down the mug.

"So what do you do all day?"

"Listen, you need a place to hang your hat for a week. Fine.
It doesn't include chatter."

He stares at her until she sticks her nose into the cup,

the heat spreading across her face. What a bitch, he's thinking, rigid old hag. Well, tough. All day long at work she makes
small talk, usually about other people's troubles. That's a
relief. If she doesn't want to exchange words with him, she
doesn't have to. Already, though, she feels sorry for the harsh
tone of her voice.

"I'm not used to having anyone here." The handwriting's on
the wall. She'll spend her mornings in the bedroom with the
door closed. It's only a week.

"I don't do well in the A.M. myself, except today I was
hatching a plot and it woke me up." He peers at her and she
can't tell if he's joking.

"My old pal Frankie's returning to the 'Nam today. He
doesn't want a send-off, but I was thinking, why do I listen
to him?"

She shrugs, always fond of Frankie. How many tired nights
did he visit Nick to relieve her from going?

"The man may have to wait at the airport for hours. Even if
the plane's on time, he's bound to be early, and all alone."

If Sean weren't Frankie's friend, he wouldn't even be here.

"We should see him off."

"I work."

"All I need is a car. If I take a bus, train, whatever, he'll be
gone before I show my face. Can I borrow yours for a few
hours?"

She stares at him. The first new car she's ever owned. She
just had it washed, serviced. No one else drives it. What if
he takes off with it? Bangs it up? "I keep it in a garage during
the week."

"Is that a rule?"

"I only use it on weekends."

"It's falling apart?"

"It's brand-new."

"I'm a careful man. No more than thirty in the city. I've never been in an accident. Want to see my license?"

"I don't even let my children drive it."

"I wouldn't either. They think they're immortal."

"Maybe, but it doesn't mean they haven't gone through shit."

"Wow, lady, I really touched the wrong button, didn't I?"

Her children have watched their father dying for years. Billie once bought him a fifth of bourbon to down his pills. The easiest way. Go out drunk. But after the second drink, an orderly took the bottle away. So what's a car? It can be replaced. "I'll leave you the keys." She walks toward the bedroom. "Tell Frankie I said take care."

▪ The car makes him uneasy. He hasn't driven in three years. Nicole was eleven. They were going to the beach. Next birthday, she'll be fourteen. And where will he be? He ought to phone her, but he hates it when Aristotle picks up, when Aristotle tells him things about Nicole he wouldn't otherwise know. Maybe he'll borrow the car again. Catch Nicole outside her school. Before the war, he used to love driving. But steering that big track, he was a turtle inside a shell, and every car since feels light as a piece of tin. Still, he's not letting Frankie prowl those slippery floors by himself. His eyes slide from the mirror to the line of cars ahead. It's TWA at JFK. He's almost sure of that. The bar? The waiting area? Nah. Most likely he's walking his soles off. Shouldn't be hard to find.

Lucy probably doesn't even believe he's going to surprise Frankie. Too caring for a man. A vet. Yeah. The woman was never in war, that's all. Caring was it. He loves Trackman, his old buddy. The skinny geezer made it through a lot of fire, but returning now is just plain crazy. Clearing mines? Stomping over old territory? If it was a job, if it paid, he still couldn't go back. Not for love, beans, or even money. How many times has he wanted to call Frankie and ask, how come? I mean, how come you're doing this? They already got your time, why give them the rest of it? Frankie, who saved his ass one million times at least, he should have tried to stop him. He has to keep him from setting foot on that plane.

Shit. He can't even afford a bottle for them to share words over. Ten friggin' bucks. That's all he has on him. Another five in his bedroom that he should have pocketed before he left.

The old fingers don't move as quickly as they used to, or he'd pop into some store and snag him some sauce. If he'd been thinking, he might have found something at Lucy's. That house didn't look dry to him. Coffee. He'll buy him coffee. He has to buy him something. You don't go out to the airport empty-handed.

Ahead on the bridge the cars bunch up. He sees the sign above the toll booths. $3.50. How many alarms would go off if he just drove through? Man, being broke stinks. He'll start hauling boards with Rod next week, but it'll take five days after that to see any greens.

A thick cloud of yellowish haze amputates the tops of the buildings across the river in Manhattan. The height of the bridge bothers him. He presses on the gas pedal. The cars ahead divide into several lanes. He moves to the left, there's room to travel. If he brings this heap back with a scratch on it, he'll be sleeping in Central Park tonight, and Lucy, sure as shit, will point the way. An argument with her will not turn out well. A very definite lady. He slows to thirty. Following the rest of the traffic, he wheels off the road, onto the expressway.

The road into the airport is nearly clear and he drives right through to a parking lot, grabs a ticket from the machine, wondering how the hell he'll pay that. As he leaves the lot, he glances in car windows. Sometimes people leave money in strange places. He could pick a lock. But first things first.

The sign reads, "TWA—INCOMING." He whistles softly. "Yeah, now that's Arrivals." He finds "Departures," steps up to the doors. They part, and he plunges into the air-conditioning, scanning the long lines of people waiting to check baggage. No Frankie. He glares at the monitor. Two flights leaving for LA. Gate 15, 11:00 A.M. Gate 19, 2:30 P.M. He heads toward gate 15, eyes peeled, checking out the cocktail lounge on the way. All the time getting closer to security, wondering what his plan is. The damn punks wear guns now. How to bullshit a gun, he isn't sure.

"Your ticket, sir?" A boy young enough to be his son holds his hand out. A son with a gun. Same age as he was then. No, he doesn't like the idea. The guard's staring at him, impatient.

"I'm just meeting a friend. Probably went through already."

"Sorry, sir, you can't pass without a ticket."

"Look." He rotates his palms like a magician. "Nothing here. Run that gadget up and down me, see if I make noise. I just need to catch my old buddy. Old buddy. Get it? There's no rule to separate friends, is there? This is an airport, right? Not a prison? This is a free country, right?" He hears his voice louder than he wants it to be. Knob on the damn volume's stuck. The boy's face doesn't help either. It reads, crazy old loon. "You understand me, son? I need to find my friend at gate fifteen." He steps forward.

The guard lifts a walkie-talkie from his belt.

"Hey, now. Let's not spread bad news. I mean no harm. Just want to do what's right. My friend's in there all alone. I can't be out here wasting good time with you."

The guard looks around. No help in sight.

"Don't press no buttons, son, don't start no wars. Everything's under control. I'm just going to find my pal. No sweat. I'll meander on through that frame. You won't hear a sound. In a minute you won't even see me. I was never here."

"I'll page your friend. What's his name?" The walkie-talkie to his mouth.

He ought to toss that little toy across the room. But whatever this boy doesn't know about live-and-die friendships he sure as hell isn't going to teach him now. Suddenly, his stomach clenches. "Yeah, good idea. Name's Frankie Bower." He moves into a nearby chair. He drops his head a few inches, letting his hands hang loosely between his knees the way the medics taught him. His stomach begins to relax. Shit. He could've thrown up all over that poor boy, no taller than Victor Charlie. Boy needs to grow. Maybe he will.

Waiting for the heat to leave his face, he listens to the page, hoping Frankie will appear so that the guard can see he's not crazy. Except he is. When he least expects it. He lifts his head, knowing he's watched, wondering what else is being piped into that walkie-talkie.

He looks around for a clock. Nowhere. Unbelievable in an airport. Better no time than the wrong time. He waits.

Turkey man's nowhere in sight. A man in Bermuda shorts emerges from the security area. The guard's eyes are on him. He jumps up, raising a clenched fist. "Hey, friend?" The stranger glances at him, walks faster. He follows until they're both out of the guard's view, then ducks into a telephone booth. Now what? Hang out? Watch the doors open and close. He has twenty minutes before his parking begins costing more than he can pay. The doors part and he's out, already composing his letter.

Dear Frankie,

Lest you think I am not thoughtful, let me share with you my trip to JFK to search you out. Would've truly enjoyed seeing your face express surprise and joy at seeing my face. But

Trackman, I am not a simple man. I am a thief, a liar, and a cheat. Sometimes. And the truth is, I went there to keep you from getting on that plane. I had no plan. Wasn't even carrying handcuffs. Only a trunkful of words. Now, you know me. I do not partake in such conversations unless I am clearly drunk or very concerned. Maybe devoted is the word. I can't imagine you humping those narrow streets and muddy roads again. I mean, man, we did it, right? I fear you're traveling there with false assumptions. One, that you can make right everything that was wrong, and/or two like they used to say in the old New Ritz bar, that some of the hair from the dog that bit you will do the trick. Man, that's booze they're talking about, that's a hangover they're curing, not three hundred and sixty-five days of shit piling into our eyeballs.

Trackman, I know you want some peace of mind. Too late. We forfeited that. You're going to laugh. I once considered becoming a monk. Like the two we met in Thailand. A long retreat where I expected nothing and no one expected anything from me. Actually, the idea was a fleeting one. At heart (or at bottom, heh, heh), I'm too itchy to keep myself tucked away.

Anyway, you eluded me at the airport—or, another way of seeing it, I wasn't meant to stop you from your journey. Therefore, I hope that when your feet touch that juicy, coffee-colored sludge, all of the old devils will be transformed into beautiful young women. And then you can get a good night's sleep. Right? You can even say hello to the boy I left behind. What I mean is, don't forget we came home old. Sincerely, Sandwich, or maybe, Yours, Sean.

The smell of gasoline from a long line of waiting taxis. Surely one of these cabbies can tell him how to get back into Manhattan without paying a toll.

▪ Walking past the open-doored offices on the first floor, Lucy hears women calling out to each other. The computers are click-clacking, faxes beep, phones ring. Ordinary activities anywhere. But normality is the subterfuge, the way to keep the respirators secret, to staunch the moans from the floors above.

It always looks the same to her, stepping off the large elevator on eight, no matter what time of day. A slightly overexposed photograph; white-clad figures imprinted on a charcoal backdrop; buttery light shining through hallway windows from tawny bed lamps; aides arranging wheelchairs like merchants setting out wares; patients groping around each other. Sometimes, if she stands still, the nurses seem to levitate in their ever-forward movements. Doctors nowhere to be seen. They sneak in and out between dawn and 9:00 A.M. So Nick tells her. In all the years of coming here, she's never surprised one tending him. She's phoned several in their private practices, where they treat real patients who pay, recover, and refer others.

It's why she visits often. The staff knows her. She won't allow them to overlook his basic needs, although he doesn't complain the way he did when he believed he'd get well.

In the dayroom, she waves to the cluster of vets in wheelchairs watching TV, the volume loud. Nick's not there, so she heads toward the great wraparound deck, really a screened-in fire escape with steps winding down to the street.

Careful not to let her clothing touch the mesh wire lest it pick up fine black lines of soot, she steps hesitantly along the narrow path. Still savoring the few moments before she sees his thinning dark hair, his narrow shoulders listing to the right, the back of his wheelchair. He was a tall boy once. Twenty-six years ago. They were married before he shipped out and had a few healthy years after he returned, before the joints inflamed and weakened, before the pain and the slowness, before they took any of it seriously. She sighs, bracing herself for the performance that's about to begin. Maybe she can do something different before the girl, that girl, that mythical girl comes into his gunsights. Gathering her energy, she bends over. "It's me," and kisses his forehead, then pulls up one of the lightweight plastic chairs, scratched and yellowed. Sitting down beside him, she places her hand on his cool, bluish fingers.

"Hello, Lucy." He stares ahead.

She feels an odd sense of relief simply because it hasn't yet begun. She can still say anything. She stares with him at the roofs of the gray stone apartment buildings, six or seven stories high, a convention of pigeons along the distant eave.

"Remember Sean Metcalf?" she asks, grabbing at a subject that might lead them elsewhere.

"Frankie's friend?"

"Thanks to Ida, he's staying at our place for a week. I'm not thrilled."

"Not our place, Lucy, yours. I've never seen it."

"You will."

"I don't want to."

"Nick!"

"What's the point?" He takes a deep breath, swallows. "It's a good idea, good for Sean, good for you."

"Me?" She lets go of his hand. She feels indignant, defensive.

"Company for you."

"I work all day with people."

"Whatever you say. You're the CO for the deal?"

Clearly, he's finished with her topic. "I brought you the booze." Already she's pouring two inches of bourbon into a paper cup, the jar still hidden inside her bag.

He drinks quickly. Holds out the cup for a refill.

"You don't owe me anything," he says.

"Owe you?" So it's starting. God, isn't there some way to stop him?

"You've taken care of business." He takes a long drink, closing his eyes. "I'd be a fool to tell you what to do. Any more stuff?"

She detects a slight slur in his speech, but pours in the last few ounces, then holds up the empty jar for him to see. "Should we go inside?"

"Too many boring stories. It's the worst thing about being here, chewing up the past until there's no juice left. Damn memories."

Oh, shit, she thinks, here it comes. "Do you want me to wheel you around out here?"

He shakes his head. "Damn memories," he repeats. "That room in Penang that had gold braiding around the door and paper lanterns covering the bulbs."

Nothing to surprise her now. "Maybe I don't want to hear this."

"Sure you do, you always want to hear everything."

The booze makes him talkative. And she brings it. How could she not?

"There's one little bed, I mean little, like a child's bed or a cot, and open windows, with lots of noise. When they're closed, the noise sounds no farther away."

"Okay, Nick. Your great R&R. Five days of fun and fucking. Do I really need to hear the details again?"

"Penang's a small island." He looks straight ahead. "I had to take a ferry there. Busy place, once you're on it. More like a city. People smiling at me like they knew me." He takes a deep breath. The pigeons scatter upward, then relocated along the same eave. The sun hides behind layers of white clouds.

"Five fabulous days. Saved my life. Made me feel human again. Clean and human. Loving and human. Human and human." He turns to her.

Even if it was true, that girl's no girl anymore, she's middle-aged, too. Tell him that, I dare you. She ought to just get up and go. He can't come after her. Ever again. That's why she's his captive audience. For how long? she wonders, feeling a certain shame at the thought.

"Her name was Su. After I returned to my platoon, I couldn't stop thinking about her. I went to see her again before I left. I was short-time and having these headaches, bad ones I couldn't sleep through. They gave me a few days off. I hopped a plane to Malaysia."

"You can stop there, Nick, I know the story."

"She mixed powders into my tea. The pain went away." With effort, he wheels around to face her. His eyes red-rimmed. The stubble on his cheek is already white. "I'm a bastard."

"You bet."

"Mad, are you?"

"Furious." Her voice tired.

"Know why I went back to her?"

"Enough."

"With just thirty days left, I realized the joke. I mean 364 days or 2, it only takes one bouncing Betty to blow you away. I could have gotten it walking across the DZ to the chopper. The plane could have gotten it before it reached the clouds. Anything could have killed me. There was no hiding. I told Su. She didn't understand everything I said, but she felt my fear in my body and she talked to me nonstop in her way. I'm eternally grateful."

"So am I," Lucy snaps. "Grateful, absolutely grateful. I ought to send her a thank-you note." These words aren't in the script, at least not so far.

He looks at her with sleepy eyes. "Something did get me," he says, "it shot me down in the skies over America. Just a few years too late to tell Su about."

Okay, so she's broken some superstitious need of his to have the usual last words. Without them, will his bad luck get any worse? She can't cause him any more angst. None of this is his fault. What is it she usually says here? She roots around in her mind. "Why are you telling me this now?"

"I don't want to be your excuse." His head drops toward his shoulder.

She walks to the screen, picks up the grinding noise of a car alarm, peers down into the darkening streets below. She needs to go home.

His eyes are closed. She stares at him until she hardly recognizes him at all, the way a word repeated too many times will turn on you.

When she emerges from the subway, only the tops of the tall buildings are bathed in the pink light of the evening sun. She takes a deep breath. She's on the edge of a headache, her limbs are heavy. Maybe she'll take a long bath. Shit. She won't be alone. Unless Sean's stolen her car. Right now, that almost sounds like an attractive scenario.

In the hallway, she hears the faint rattle of TV voices behind forest-green doors. She jams her key in the lock. Music. It's him. Letting the door slam shut, she kicks off her shoes. Smells food cooking.

"Hello," he calls.

She doesn't answer.

"I'm preparing dinner."

With her food?

"Rice dish . . . à la Sean." His jovial tone sounds forced. The wise thing would be to plead tiredness, go straight to her room. Except it's her kitchen.

Her eyes go to the counter littered with diced tomatoes, broccoli, carrots, squash. He's perched on a stool at the counter chopping something that could be celery or the end of a scallion. This on a wooden cutting board he could only have found by looking through every one of her cupboards.

"Are you preparing for an army?" Her orderly kitchen, a mess. He's left everything out, on display, cabinet doors ajar, drawers half open.

"Leftovers can be frozen."

"Make sure to clean this." She can't help herself. She always straightens up as she cooks. "You should have mentioned your plans to me."

"Why?"

"I would've discouraged them."

"Too late." He smiles without merriment, and she walks away, scanning surfaces for her car keys. Where did he get the money anyway? He's supposed to be broke.

In the bedroom she undresses carefully, hanging up her clothes. Mustn't think, just do. She eyes her sweats. A run would be good for her mood. What is her mood? She chooses a pair of shorts, changes her mind, reaches deep into her closet for the long batik lounger Nick bought her years ago. Lets it drop. Pulls on her sweats. Then sits in the rocking chair, her feet on the bed. She needs to calm down.

She doesn't like him taking over, but a mess can be cleaned up. Still, it's not his house. He's a guest. She's not used to this. She's in charge. Perhaps too long. If Nick had been well, it would have been different. She'd be different, but she can't imagine how. Not anymore. She pads into the living room where he's setting the table.

"Is the car back in the garage?"

"Nope. I left it on the Triborough Bridge." He pours himself a glass of wine.

She looks at him.

"Lord, lord, lady, I'm kidding. Mission scrapped."

"You didn't go?"

"Couldn't find Mr. Trackman. Probably left from Newark. Yeah, car's in the garage. Keys in the kitchen. It didn't rain. No one sideswiped it. I didn't use the ashtray. It's possible a gum wrapper blew inside. I can have the car vacuumed this weekend. Relax. Have a glass of wine."

She shakes her head. It's his wine and she doesn't want it. Where'd he get money for wine? She wants scotch. Later, when she's alone. But she won't be alone. She'll take the bottle into the bedroom.

From the recliner, she watches him moving around her kitchen as if he'd lived there all his life.

"So there I was at the airport." He places a large dish of rice in the center of the table. "And no Frankie."

"Did you page him?"

"Matter of fact, I did. It's just as well." He brings in the bowl of sautéed vegetables, begins filling her plate.

"So how's Nick?"

"Fine."

"Fine?"

"I don't want to talk about it."

"What do you want to talk about?"

"Nothing."

"Can't you even fake being nice to me?"

"Why should I?"

"Manners."

"I don't have any."

"Hey, I know you're doing me a favor, but don't treat me like I'm soiling your space. All right? I'm out of here in a week."

"Where to?" Her tone low.

He looks at her. "Rod and Emma's for a while." Once again he refills his glass. So wine's his Achilles' heel. They all have one, don't they?

"Do you use the park?" he asks.

"Excuse me?"

"Central Park? Do you run there?"

"Not after dark."

He peers at her. Perhaps he needs glasses. Probably doesn't even read. She does, every night. Two drinks and her book. It's the only way to unwind, the only way to fall asleep. A ritual begun long ago. Scotch hidden in milk in case the children woke up. She pushes the food around her plate. Lifts a forkful into her mouth.

"How is it?"

"Don't watch me."

"You're nice to watch."

What does he want now?

"How about a walk? Show me the sights."

The vegetables, diced and colorful, are like confetti on her rice.

"In Central Park."

"At night?" His eyes are too bright. "I can't. I have paperwork to do."

She waits for him to ask her another question, the silence stangely discomforting. "How's Tess?"

"Ask her new husband."

"I don't know him."

"He owns a diner. Tess is with him all day. You enjoy your job?"

"Beats haircutting."

"Is that what you used to do?"

She nods, avoiding those too-active eyes. "What about you?"

"Me? I can't seem to find work that doesn't short-fuse my intestines."

"What can you do?"

"Fix cars, build cabinets, carve wood, invent toys, imper-sonate great chefs. I also shoot men." He bows his head, shov-els in the food.

The clock with its delicate golden hands reads 7:50. In a little while the sun will set. Her eyes slide to the window, where the light has changed from pink to mauve, then back to his half-empty plate. "You cooked. I'll clean up."

He finishes the wine. "Okay. I'll wander around for a bit." He pushes back his chair.

At the door, he stares at her, hands on his hips. Then he's out and she thinks of cowboys in westerns. And, maybe, if she lets her mind wander, sagebrush under a gentle evening light. But movies are make-believe.

▪ Cars whiz by. His body hugs the stone wall. The narrow sidewalk leads east through Central Park to Fifth Avenue. Lucy should have accepted, not left him out here alone. The lady's too edgy by half, though living with someone like her could be a relief. She takes care of herself, stands on her own two feet. Probably doesn't need a man at all. He has an edge, too. It comes from the wine and he wants to keep it.

He leaves the park, the street, graying. Going downtown on Madison Avenue, he avoids eyes, looks into a few store win-dows with sumptuous offerings. Sees one emerald bracelet. What could a hit-and-run thief get for that? He could drop it on Lucy's dressing table, if she has one, but actually he doesn't favor bejeweled women, or golden-armed gals as Frankie calls them. By now turkey man's plane is high in the sky. And when that bird glides into the landing space and settles down like a sheet losing wind, there'll be no more run-ning across the pad wondering if it's all going to end before the party begins. This time Frankie can stand there and take a long look around. His own eyes never left straight ahead. Damn tree line still walks through his dreams.

At Seventy-ninth Street, he goes into a deli for a take-out cup of coffee. It's too hot to hold. He pours the liquid into a manhole, keeps the cup. He could park outside the Whitney Museum. But it's too bright. Step into the spotlight, ladies and gents, and let me show you some magic. I raise this cup, turn my head and, presto, the cup's full.

The church is the place, he decides, passing the museum entrance. A well-shaven, cleanly dressed man like him could be the deacon. Certainly, one of the flock. It's the contrast. People see him there, arm outstretched. A sight to ponder, not simply to pass by. He'll do well near God's house as long as he's a little high. As long as he doesn't look into anyone's eyes.

A blanket covers the sky, decorated by a smoky sliver of moon. The church takes up half of Seventy-first Street. Long marble steps lead up to large wooden doors, framed by black bands of steel. Two recessed, arched, street-level doorways are deep enough for sleeping. But he'll be out of here before anyone needs to use them. Lucky him. He has Lucy. Well, not exactly. But her sweet domain. She must have a boyfriend somewhere. It's not possible that she's sleeping alone after so many years.

He surveys the wide arc of steps and chooses the bottom one for the convenience of others. He looks inside the cup. It's almost dry. Facing away from Lucy's place, he holds it out.

Frankie will be sleeping in the City of Ho tomorrow night. No tents. Barracks gone. Darkness, absolute.

A man tucks money into the cup and passes, walking quickly, as glad as him not to lock eyes. A buck. That deserves a "God bless" or "Have a nice evening," but he's too chicken to even say "Thank you." Some people find it easy to give away small change, but not the big stuff. No one gives that away easily.

He drops down, sets the cup next to his knee, feels the edge of the step between his fingers the way he once did the water-worn rocks at Jones Beach. Another lifetime.

He hears the thud of coins against the folded bill inside the cup. Turns his head without raising it. Sees loafers, jeans, a woman's long, slim legs going up the street, the tips of straight brown hair touching shoulder blades under a thin T-shirt. Then she turns the corner.

A young woman of some means, entering, he guesses, a door held open by a uniformed man, and another who rides her up to the best floor, the penthouse floor.

He looks into the cup. Two quarters. She walks around with less than him. All her cash tied up in stocks and bonds. Charges whatever she needs, everywhere she goes.

He picks up the cup, crosses to the opposite side of the church. His edge is fading. Beggars need to be tanked up. That's the rule. It's what his buddies have told him. Fill them up and watch them dance. Maybe Lucy dances. In her dreams. He should have followed Miss Loafers. Probably has a bar-room with stools and mirrors and pretzels and crystal glasses. Even a bartender. No bouncer, though. Just nice sofas along the back wall for those who find the stools too lonely.

Why not follow her? Women like him. She probably has plenty of energy. That's a good fact. She'll expect him to cater to her. That's a bad fact. Except he'll turn on the wit. She'll laugh with her mouth open. Too bad they had to meet this way. Jesus. He stares into the cup. The magic of oblivion, he had it this afternoon. Made nearly twenty dollars. Too much to ask for twice in a day.

He scoops out the money, tosses the cup into a trash bin, lopes up Madison, dropping the cash into another sucker's cup.

"Thank you."

"Always like to help out when I can."

The beggar's eyes are on him as he continues his stride. So that's what it feels like. Makes a man top dog. Shit. He'd like to fill all the cups on all the streets of this damn city. Grow back his beard. White, like a real Santa. Except he doesn't even have a reindeer, not one, baby, and that means walking home. To Lucy's. Dark-haired lady.

He reaches the park entrance. He has to get across that dark, tree-lined space without thinking he's somewhere else. He runs, full speed, eyes straight ahead. New York's full of crazy bastards, and he's one of them.

▪ She wipes the last dish, returns it carefully to the cupboard. Surveys the tidy kitchen. Nothing left to do. She pours scotch into her milk and parks herself in the living room. Through the wall of windows the night and sky wrap a dark curve around the well-lit room. This is her favorite spot. The world at a distance.

She takes a long sip of her drink. What's to be done about her visits to Nick? The end of her patience is near. Today was proof. If only she were jealous, it would make the details important. After all, in his memory, that girl will never, like her, get old. Passionate boy that he was, who else did he sleep with? Maybe she'll ask. No one wants to die with their secrets. It's too lonely. But who wants to die without any? It never occurred to her to fool around while he was away. She still sleeps with a night light and the radio on low. Maybe it's good to go against one's nature. Stop doing what's expected, drop old rituals. Maybe she needs a secret.

She mixes another drink, returns to the living room to

lower the AC. She hears the key in the lock. He strides in, sweating, and stops short, his chest heaving, the false merriment of a few hours before gone from his face. He turns and walks quickly into the kitchen. He opens the fridge and grabs the wine. She watches him drink straight from the bottle. Go to bed, she tells herself, lock the door. Then with bottle in hand he disappears into the bathroom.

Who's he running from this time? Who's he mugged? Oh Lord, what has she gotten herself into? Be calm, be calm. Ida wouldn't place her in danger, and he's Frankie's friend. Still, with these guys, who knows? They can turn on you in a second. Like German shepherds.

The noise of the shower rushes into the quiet living room, then stops. Quickly finishing her drink, she steps out on the balcony, closing the door behind her. She's not ready for bed, dammit.

The dark park is dotted with lights. A warm breeze brushes her skin. A telephone rings in the next apartment. "No one's home," she mutters, because her neighbor's on vacation and she's watering the plants. Behind her, her own well-cared-for foliage arrayed on two round, glass-topped tables, made by her son. The phone stops ringing. Her neighbor, with no children, has lived twenty years in that apartment. Their pasts so different, their lives now similar.

"Have a drink with me," he orders, coming up beside her, barefoot, placing his large hands on the railing.

"No thanks."

"Why not?"

"I've had two."

"So what?"

"That's my limit."

"You have too many limits. Stay here. I'll bring out the wine."

She's about to remind him that it's her house, he's her guest, but he's gone. She promises Ida an earful tomorrow, first thing, and turns to leave. Once more he's striding toward her, holding aloft the half-empty bottle of wine and two glasses. He pushes aside some plants, arranges a makeshift bar. Pressing a glass into her hand, he closes her fingers around it. His damn eyes look right through her skull and it scares her.

She tugs away.

"Talk to me."

Inches toward the living room.

"Don't leave. What I have isn't catching." Then he laughs, and she can't tell if he's going to smack her or cry.

"Look, I need to get some sleep."

"I'd never stand in the way of what you need." He steps toward her, she backs up. He reaches around behind her, pushes open the door. She walks fast into her bedroom. Maybe he'll stay out there all night. Maybe he'll jump. She undresses, slips on her nightgown, lies down. Soon she hears him padding around the apartment. She's wide-awake herself. If he paces all night, it'll drive her crazy. She ought to have another scotch, but she'd have to go out there again.

He stops outside her door, his presence palpable. "Are you asleep?"

She has a choice. "What is it?"

"Company. I need it." His tone urgent. "Lucy?"

"Yes."

"Just a few minutes."

She can feel his mouth against the wood. God, what should she do? Move the dresser in front of the door?

"Lucy?"

"Yes."

"It's okay, I'm not crazy. Lucy?"

"I'm here."

"This door's between us. Please."

"Okay." She drags her robe from the chair, wraps it around her, belts it. When she opens the door, he seems surprised.

"Want some decaf?"

He shakes his head, but follows her into the living room anyway.

"What happened tonight?"

"Wrong question," he mumbles, and sits beside her on the couch, takes her hand. "Don't say anything. I'm very cold."

"I'll shut off the AC."

"Don't move. Please."

They're huddled together like two bone-broken people under one blanket on a park bench. Lord, what now, she thinks. Maybe if she sits here a few more minutes she can take her leave.

"You make me feel safe," he whispers. "Know what I mean?"

In a funny way, she does.

"You'd be a lucky Lucy for some guy. You take care of business, make everything solid. No holes to fall through."

Very gently, she tries to remove his hand, but he holds fast.

"Are you going to keep me here all night?"

"Just a little while longer." He looks at her, his eyes startled, afraid.

"Does it hurt somewhere?"

"Not like that. Sometimes it's in my gut, but sometimes it's nowhere at all."

"Like now?"

He nods.

"Was someone chasing you?"

"In a way."

"Who was it?"

"I get anxious, that's all. Lucy?"

"What?"

He wraps both arms around her, presses her toward him. She squirms and he lets go.

"I wasn't comfortable."

"Let me try again."

"Maybe not, Sean."

"Right." He begins pacing. "I should be busy all the time," he tells her. "The way you are. I don't like being idle. I suppose I could wash dishes at some dive, but I might get stuck there. That'd be tragic. I want to hold myself out for something better, something decent, understand?"

She nods.

"When I'm busy, I get tired, I sleep better. I have no idea where Frankie's sleeping tonight. His being there makes me nervous."

"Don't think about it."

"Because I can't get the place out of my mind. That's what happened in the park. Night sounds, so near. I ran all the way. Frankie shouldn't have gone back. When it gets dark, he'll freak out. I wanted to save him, but I couldn't find him."

She's had enough of it. Sean's war, Nick's war, Frankie's war. She's the one who needs a little R&R. No one sent her out for five days of fun and fucking. "Frankie's doing just what he wants to do. Good night, Sean." As she walks toward the bedroom, he intercepts her.

"Let's get into bed together. No fooling around. Just warmth. Body to body. I'm going to try another shower. If your door's ajar, I'll come in. Don't answer now."

She closes the bedroom door behind her, takes off her robe, lies flat on the bed staring at the ceiling. That would be insane. Then again, who would know? What people do in their own homes is their business. Her children are gone. She can do what she wants. She glances at the door. He'll go to bed, so will she, and that'll be that. No doubt the best thing.

The phone rings. She lets the answering machine pick it

up. It's probably her son in California, forgetting the time difference again. For him the night's just beginning.

She steps out of bed, straightens the top sheet, tucking it in, shuts off the night light, carefully opens the door a crack. She's lying on her side, her arm stuffed under the pillow, eyes open when she hears him enter the room.

"Where did you get all that food money today?"

"Standing in front of a church."

She's staring hard at the spot on the dresser where the family photos undoubtedly are.

"So I panhandle and you're not friendly, so none of us are perfect." He moves in beside her, his belly touching her back. She curls her legs. His knees fit inside hers. His arm wraps her waist. She can't remember how Nick felt against her, only that his chin would rest on her head. The clothing he'll never wear again, Sean can have it. Get rid of those cheap jeans.

8. THE THINGS WE DO TO
MAKE IT HOME

SARA-JO / MILLIE

■ It's not even a gallery, just a converted storefront. A dump, really. Cracks in the ceiling, warped wooden floors, a few metal folding chairs. Serge's photos are mounted on a pukey green baize, illuminated only by track lights. How gross. She expected at least a loft, with some good-looking people milling around. But there's only one thin young man sitting behind a small desk. He smiles weakly at her. Sara-Jo lifts some fingers in response, then drops her backpack onto a chair and begins studying the black-and-white images.

Men in trailers, tents, trucks, cars. Men sleeping on benches, lounging on grass, huddled in doorways. Men in tattered coats, stained pants, worn fatigues. Men with vacant stares over laughing mouths, noses poking past heavy beards, foreheads lined and shiny. A wall of vets vacationing from life, maybe even her father. Wouldn't that be a laugh? Except she's not in a fun mood.

On the adjacent wall, beaches and bruised skies. Rocky coasts, sandy coasts, low tide, high tide, rain, sun. No people. No boats. Not even a lighthouse. Depressing. What's he trying for? The vet photos give her the creeps, too. A waste of time and money and film. Nothing uplifting. Nothing bigger than life. Not a face here she'd trust. Not a man who could take care of anyone. Even Millie wouldn't like these. Of course, her mother's not the photo type. That's Ida's thing, a closetful of albums. She ought to show Serge Ida's pictures, if it's vets he wants to see.

Glaring at the images, she's caught by the pale, manic eyes of a man too old for the Mohawk he sports. Rooster's eyes are crazy, too. Any one of them with his eyes closed, that would be a prize shot. Serge should have consulted her. Teaching the teacher. He wouldn't like that. He thinks she's too young to know anything. He'll learn.

She should have toked up before coming. These are photos that should only be seen through the glow of a high. When Millie found her smoking once, she said being high was ugly. "Crude" was her word, "crude." But her mother doesn't understand. She's tough, not crude. She's smooth, polished, sophisticated, or soon to be all of the above. She rummages her pockets for a stick of gum. Maybe she'll crack the door for a bit of air. Maybe not, maybe she'll leave.

Once more she runs her eyes over the photos, wanting to see these men, truly see them, when they can't watch her. She has an urge to blacken their eyes into patches. Rogues captured by her and sentenced to spend their time making others happy. And if they can't, they can go straight to hell.

She hoists the backpack onto her shoulder. Too heavy, his whole approach. She'll tell him that. After she tells him she's been here.

▪ The faces in the mall belong to strangers. No one Millie's ever spoken to. No one to whom she can say, I've just come from the doctor, the news is bad. Even her daughter is three thousand miles away.

A young woman runs past her, hair and breasts bouncing. She's tempted to shout, Don't rush, life is short. She wanders down pink steps beside a strawberry-colored fountain. She knows she can't return to work.

Her car is in sector H3 under a vast orange square in the endless parking lot, one insect among many. Although it's hot and the air's full of grit, she rolls down the windows.

The road is a sizzling swath of asphalt. Around her the Sierras rise steeply. Her throat's dry, as it usually is in this place of no humidity with sky wherever she looks. Sara-Jo's letter is open on the seat beside her.

The Joshua trees in their tortuous poses line the streets on the way into town like so many statues. She turns up a narrow, winding lane through two stone columns and onto an estate that rises lush and green like a rain forest. Barking, the rottweiler sprints toward the car, landing two brown-tipped paws on the window ledge. She pats its wrinkled forehead, then touches the gas and creeps past the sprawling adobe mansion to park on a spit of gravel shaded by two banyan trees.

The dog prances after her as she hikes up the path to Pete's white stucco cottage. The estate is huge. A caretaker could be anywhere, working at one of a hundred chores. He wants her to move in with him, but the place is too primitive, too small, too inhospitable to femaleness.

Reaching the cottage first, the dog looks at her regretfully, then begins nosing its way back down the path. It belongs to Ernest, the son of the owner, and knows where its bread is buttered. The owner's son. She hears herself telling it, the way she still tells so much to herself in this fantastic land, as if only a constant voice-over could remind her she's actually here. Pete doesn't own much of anything, it's saying. No TV, not even a phone. He loves simplicity, thinks of it as a kind of freedom. He's not responsible for anyone but himself. At the moment, that feels selfish to her. Maybe she should have gone straight into town, found herself a travel agent and bought a ticket to New York.

The door is wide open, sunlight dappling the cool, dark interior. But no Pete. She walks around back and sits in the canvas chair. It'll be cold in New York. She'll need a coat. And Lucy's moved. To an apartment she's never seen. What if Lucy doesn't have room? They could share a bed, of course. She smiles at the absurdity—and the familiarity—of the thought. As children, poor little girls that they were, they shared the pullout in the living room where the light from the streetlamp poured in like a midnight sun.

She hears Pete's whistle. He's coming up the hill. Long, shaggy, straw-yellow hair, naked shoulders, thick legs in cut-off jeans, bare feet. He's ten years younger than she and stronger than any man she's ever known. He doesn't hurry, searching her face for signs.

"It's positive," she says.

"Millie, it's nothing but a temporary setback." He drops to the ground, his gray eyes steady on her. "What else did they say?"

"The doctors want to do a bunch of tests."

"Then?"

"Surgery."

"How do you know they're right?"

"It's there." She touches her pelvis. But she doesn't believe it either, can't even say the word aloud.

"I'll find you a drink."

"I got a letter from Sara-Jo," she calls after him. She's read it three times. They don't talk much anymore. Phoning's expensive—and then there's something else, something she can't put her finger on, something that makes her hesitate to return, even with cancer. The cottage is now in half-shadow, the sun slipping like an egg yolk between the two mountains.

Pete plants the bamboo tray on the tree stump he's smoothed into a table. A bottle of Jim Beam, a jug of water, a bowl of ice. He knows what she likes. He mixes her a drink, handing her the glass. He raises his old tin Sierra cup. "To you and the future," he says quietly. She knows it's only water. To keep her company. He never touches liquor.

"I wish I didn't have to tell Sara-Jo."

"She'd never forgive you if you didn't."

He's right. She likes that. "I'm thinking about going back to New York for the operation." She can hear the hesitation, the shakiness in her voice.

"Why?"

"Everyone's there." The familiars will rise around her like the sides of a crib. But is that what she wants? Is that what she needs?

"It doesn't make sense, Millie."

"Because you want me here." She hears the words and something that sounds almost like bitterness in them.

"Of course I do." Irritation lowers his voice. He has no patience for the obvious—or for her uncertainty.

She can feel herself trembling. Life is so clear to him. At her age even answers don't lay questions to rest. "Maybe it's what I need?"

"Here you won't be stuck indoors because of weather. I'll cook, change dressings. There's nothing like that for you back there, and I know you know that."

It's Rooster who wanders into her mind now. Despite

herself. Despite everything. How strange. But he's not the reason, he can't be. Maybe once, when she was so much younger than Pete and he was still beautiful, but not anymore, not now. "My daughter, my sister are there," she recites mechanically. Lucy would prefer her in New York, wouldn't she? But not Sara-Jo, who doesn't want a full-time mother on her case or a full-time case for a mother.

"I can't see you in some New York City hospital."

But that's just what she sees: the biggest, best, most modern facility to give her certainty, and a world all around her that she knows the way she knows how to breathe. It's hopeless, she's aware of that. Pete can't understand. He still feels immortal. She never has and so will take whatever assurance there is.

"Let's walk." He leads her up the path behind the cottage; it is filled with the dark, cool scent of eucalyptus. "I'll share the experience with you."

"It's not an experience, Pete, it's a disaster."

"It doesn't have to be."

"Don't go touchy-feely on me, please."

But he's plucking some wildflowers, almost as if to mock her, leaving the harshness of her voice to hang in the air. "You won't let me comfort you," he mutters and stalks ahead, not even offering her the flowers as she had somehow hoped.

She hurries to catch up to him, she's breathing hard when she says, "Pete, I have cancer. I don't know what's coming. Nothing seems the same as yesterday. It's already changed. And I don't even know how."

His finger follows the flight of a Steller's jay, its head an iridescent blue-black in the sunlight.

"In New York you'll see pigeons," he says.

"I'll be locked away in some hospital wherever I am."

"You're giving in to this too quickly."

"There's a tumor inside me and telling you about it isn't relieving me."

"Will your family do that?"

"I don't know."

"Then why are you going back?"

She walks beside him, head down. The things he's saying feel so young. What could she possibly say in reply?

"You feel fine."

She feels terrible and they're family, they're the ones who have to take care of her if she doesn't get well. Someday she'll explain all this to him, even what she doesn't now understand. "There's something inside me," she repeats in a monotone.

"You didn't know that until they told you."

"Is that why you never go to doctors?"

"It's not who you see, it's how you think about what they tell you."

"If I don't think of myself as a woman with cancer, then I'm not?"

She hears footsteps. The dog leaps ahead of Ernest and presses two paws against her chest.

"Down, Zephyr," Pete orders. The dog sits, panting. Ernest is older than Pete and half his size. He's tan, smooth-shaven, with a pouting mouth and sullen eyes that threaten anyone who dares to show pity.

"Nice and cool right here." Ernest rocks back and forth on his heels, a pretense of ease. He reminds her in some odd way of Rooster, who mastered the art of disengagement so well he could disappear while still talking to her. Sara-Jo saw that right away. Children do. It took her longer, almost a lifetime. Almost a lifetime. She repeats it to herself until she can taste the bitterness in the words.

"My tarot cards told me you had no plans for dinner, so I ordered the cook to prepare food for three on the lawn at six.

The tarot cards also warned me not to eat alone tonight." He tries a smile, curling his lips briefly to reveal some teeth but no pleasure.

"We'll think it over," Pete tells him.

"Don't take too long, the food will get cold." He walks away, the dog loping after him.

"Was that a threat or an invitation?" she asks.

"He's lonely."

"I'm not surprised."

"He's semiharmless."

"Semi?"

"When he's here. Out in the world I'm not so sure."

"But he always sounds this way."

"What way?" He takes her hand.

"Like he masturbates with a grenade in each pocket."

"If he does, he doesn't tell me about it. Listen, let's sleep outside tonight."

All she can imagine is soft hotel beds and an ice machine down the hall, but somehow she can't bring herself to say that, to highlight their differences more, and so just says, "With him on the prowl?" Although Ernest scares her not at all.

"He won't be."

"He just was."

"He had to find us to invite us."

"Are you afraid to say no to him?"

"He doesn't have friends. I'm just here, part of his world. The last time he asked me to dinner they had taken his father off to the hospital. That was a year ago."

"But his father's back."

"So it's something else. Who knows? It's just a meal. An hour."

An hour, she thinks, again tasting the bitterness. "Why are you friends with him anyway?" She hears Sara-Jo's sullen tone in hers.

"We're the flip sides of each other. War and peace. You can't have one without the other. He came back here after that war ended and never left again."

"Not a bad place to come back to." The war disconnected Rooster's insides, too, but in their small apartment where could he roam? "You were saved from all that. Just a baby, then."

"That's what they tell me."

"You feel no connection to that time, do you?"

"Why should I?"

"History," she says, because she, Rooster, even Sara-Jo are his history, whether he knows it or not.

He stops. His eyes fixed on her. "I'm not a category. You can't judge me by a time and place that aren't relevant to my life."

"What is relevant, then?" she asks, feeling a body inside her body sag with disappointment.

"The present, the future, you."

"That's too easy."

"Millie, drop the baggage. It gets in the way. Our way." He slides his arm around her waist.

She walks with him, suddenly weepy. By the time they reach the clearing, the sun has gone behind the mountains, leaving only a ring of tangerine haze. She falls into the hammock's strong netting, which folds around her. A warm breeze brushes her forehead, and a longing for peace overwhelms her, a longing she's had many times, a longing that brought her here. Now the sweetness of it seems like a mere tease. Place is only an extension of well-being. Pete will never accept that. She hoists herself up. "Back home," she begins, sure now that's where she's headed, "I have a friend who's a nurse, she'll make all the arrangements."

He hands her a fresh drink. She takes a sip. "Perhaps I'll come east with you," he says lightly.

Pete in New York? She can't see it. Her family, her friends, won't know what to make of him, of a life untouched by war, unravaged. They'll think him too young, too privileged, a recluse. What kind of a job does he have anyway? Worse yet, what will he make of them? Will he see them as crude? And what will that say about her? The her that he's never met, doesn't really know, that she doesn't need him to understand. And whose apartment will she have to squeeze him into? And won't the rush-hour subway drive him bananas? How long could he possibly last in the real world, her world, anyway? And what kind of example will she set for Sara-Jo? "You hate big cities."

"I'll manage."

They'll only let him visit the hospital so many hours a day, and what will he do the rest of the time? "You don't know a soul. And where would you sleep? You can't camp out in the city. And what about your work? Ernest needs you, doesn't he?" But he refuses to respond. He simply moves away from her, gathering hunks of wood, handfuls of twigs. She follows him into the cottage. He drops the wood in front of the fireplace, removes an ice tray from the fridge, empties it with a crash into the sink. His movements sharp, deliberate, each giving off the heat of anger. She knows better than to touch him now. She shouldn't have rejected his offer so quickly. Shit. Let him come. She's not responsible for him. He can take care of himself. Let him sleep in the park. She nearly laughs. God, she can't take this. She needs stroking. She has cancer. She could lose her hair. Jesus. Who cares what happens to him in New York?

She finds herself in the doorway, her back to him, the sky purpling. How did she get here? She hears herself say, "If you really want to come east . . ."

"Never mind. This is your trip." Finality, maybe even meanness in his voice. She turns. He's not looking at her. He's sprawled in the overstuffed chair, her chair, the only one that's really comfortable. She perches on the frayed wicker rocker. Maybe he doesn't care anymore. Maybe he never did. But how can that be? He extracts from her a level of pleasure that radiates back to her like the sun on water. No small feat. She has to let him care for her in his way, doesn't she? She stares at his weathered face, a badge of the life he's chosen.

"I didn't want to worry about you in the city," she begins, a half-truth at best.

"Well, you won't have to now, will you? Just send me a postcard."

"Oh shit." She drops between his knees. "Don't be angry with me."

"Not with you, with your going."

"Even if it's right for me?"

"You're thinking magically about home."

"My daughter's there."

"Trying to grow up."

"I'm letting her."

"If she was here, would you still go?"

"Don't you believe I'll return?"

"Maybe yes, maybe no." The stony anger gone now from his eyes.

"Why do you say that?"

"Back east there's a cave, it'll take time to get in, longer to get out, if you do get out again."

"You don't know me that well." Or the life she's led. "You're acting as though my going back is some planned-out process, but it's an impulse." An impulse of doom, she thinks, the same one that has her moving full vases into the middle of tables, that sends her into Sara-Jo's room to crack open the window, that has her pulling the plugs on all the appliances before leaving for work. Except, now, the worst has happened, the waiting's over. And, back home, they'll understand her dreadful relief. She takes Pete's hand. "Let's go eat."

As they take the path down, she runs her palm along the top of the stone wall, feeling the scratch of grit. Her thoughts are speeding. Already the future's erased for her. All planning is for now. But what is the plan? What if she doesn't phone Sara-Jo, doesn't go back to the doctor, doesn't have surgery, just exists here "as is," like the tag at a fire sale? Is that what Pete would like? Is that what he believes is best?

"What if I forget the whole deal? No back home, no surgery, nothing?"

"That's one option," he says carefully.

Too late. He didn't jump at her idea or even whistle his relief. He doesn't know any more than she does after all.

Ernest is already seated at a round table covered with a blue-checkered cloth. The table's set for three, with white cloth napkins, white porcelain plates, a carafe of margaritas, two long-stemmed glasses. The dog, at Ernest's feet, is tethered to a tree by a rope. This surprises her. He always roams free.

On a nearby table, several silver serving dishes rest over low candle flames.

"How's your father?" Pete asks.

"Dying every day." Ernest pours her a margarita. She sips at it, although the bourbon is still alive inside her.

"Aren't you joining me?" she asks.

"Don't smoke or drink. Walk five miles a day and swim each dawn. Everything my father never did."

"But he's ninety," Pete says.

"And sick for ten years."

"Still, that's a long life."

"What difference, if it's not a healthy one."

Who in her family ever made it to eighty? Her dad died of

a stroke at fifty, her mom at sixty-two. Rooster was a teenager when his parents died. And Sara-Jo? What will be her fate? She eyes the dog, which periodically lunges forward, each time stopped abruptly by the rope. "Why's he tied up?" she asks.

"He's sick. I'm having him put away tomorrow."

She stares at Ernest to see if he's kidding. He's not.

"Leukemia. His healthy days are over."

"You don't know that for certain." Her voice indignant. Pete's hand comes to rest lightly on her shoulder.

"This is the last time you'll see him. That's why we're having dinner together."

"Let me take him," Pete says.

"He'd be a useless pet, and I'd have to watch him deteriorate. Tomatoes have to be red. No room on the shelf for brown spots. People don't buy ugly. They can't love it."

She stares at him unblinkingly, she'd like to pummel him until he cries.

"The downturn, when it comes, can be painful. Why wait until he weakens, can't move around, can't be what he is, what he's supposed to be?"

"You're doing this for your sake, not the dog's."

"What do you know about dying? It's not pretty and often it's not quick, and nothing says I have to watch it again, and I won't."

She recognizes the I'm-done-with-suffering expression. She knows it all too well. It's futile to struggle. Even Zephyr seems to sense it. He's stopped pulling at the rope. Even if they took him deep into the woods and let him go, he'd find his way back here. "You have no right to kill that dog," she says.

"He's mine." A child stating a fact.

She leans near Pete and whispers, "I've changed my mind.

Come to New York. I need you." Then pushing back her chair, she strides up the path. Pete's probably explaining ". . . has cancer herself . . . could die . . . bad timing." She reaches the stone wall, stops to catch her breath. It's nearly dark, absolutely still, and his words have spooked her. The sooner the surgery's done, the better. She sees Pete through watery eyes. He pulls her close.

As soon as they're inside the cottage, she half sobs, "We have to get Zephyr away from him." Already she's made the dog her talisman.

"I'll try again in the morning."

"*Take* him," she implores.

"I can't steal him, Millie."

"Why not? He's going to kill the dog. He'll be without him anyway. What's the difference?"

"Stop pacing. Come here." He stretches out on the floor.

She straddles his hips, leans close to his face. "I meant what I said. I want you to come to New York. It might not turn out well. You and my family." And the guys, she thinks to herself. Always them. She can feel herself beginning to smile. Despite herself. "I'm taking a risk."

"The risk is staying here with me."

"California's not home to me."

"When Sara-Jo was little, you kissed the wound and made the pain go away. She can't do that for you."

"And you?"

"I come closest."

"Why won't you go with me, then?"

"Because you were right the first time. I'll be isolated from what makes me good for you."

She moves off him, into the comfortable chair.

"We'll bring Sara-Jo here for a visit," he says. "We have hospitals, just as high-tech, and doctors just as good as any in New York."

How tempting, she thinks. He's trying. But it's so much simpler than that. She needs to touch everyone she knows and they need to touch her before . . . in case the tie is broken. It's the right thing to do, as natural as sleeping or eating and just as involuntary. There seems to be no back home for Pete. He's already here, perhaps in a retreat of his own, and besides he's young, he's healthy. He needs another decade, two, three, twenty, to begin to understand her impulse. Her eyes slide to the braided rug, a crimson oval in front of the door, then back to his face. "I need to go home."

"You're scared, it's to be expected. Phone, tell them all about it, but don't go." He begins piling kindling in the fireplace around a balled-up sheet of newspaper.

"We're not in the same place now, you and me."

"Millie." He turns to her. "Listen to yourself. You're putting distance between us. I want you close, as close as I can get you."

"Only if I move toward you."

"I know where I function best." She hears the impatience again. His mind's made up.

"I'm going back to my place tonight." She walks to the door.

"We'll talk in the morning, then. I'll try to make Ernest see how rash he's being."

"Like me?"

"I didn't say that."

She hurries down the dark path toward the car.

▪ Sara-Jo replaces the receiver. "Shit." She doesn't want her mother sick, doesn't want her back in New York either. She would have visited California. Easily. They could have had quality time together. Not a prayer for that here. The family, these men, they'll swirl around her mother, every night a wake even though she's alive. Gather, drink, and be gross. And worse, they'll insist on including her. "Shit." With Millie gone, she's managed to keep her distance. What a relief.

Her first impulse is to call Serge. Instead she drops onto the bed, propping three pillows behind her head. She's not to phone him if it doesn't pertain to photography. She smiles despite her sudden misery. Who's he kidding? He was attracted to her the minute she entered his workshop. She could tell. Her responses amused him. She caught the glances even when he purposely turned away from her. And his pleasure. You like bleak landscapes? The flat twang. Where's he from anyway?

She looks forward to sleeping with him. He'll be passionate, in control, experienced. He's twenty-four years older. She'll have to convince him that he's not robbing the cradle, that she's not some soapy princess with an empty head. That she doesn't want to be tied to him or any man. Not now. Not ever.

Outside the day is gray, cold. Looks like snow. Not good weather for anyone to recuperate in. And why come east without Pete?

She can't remember her mother ever being sick. It occurs to her suddenly that Millie hasn't given her many details about the illness, just as she's long avoided talking much about Pete. She'd better not be protecting her.

She grabs a sweater from the chair and pulls it over her head, drawing the sleeves down to her fingertips. God, she's cold. She'd pay mightily for some dope right now, but school's closed. Vet's day. What a joke. A shot of brandy with some tea would be just right, except Ida only has bourbon, which she can't stand.

She begins to pace the tiny room. "I can't take care of Millie. I have to write essays, fill out applications." She stops in front of the mirror. "I can't get used to her being here." Wow. Already talking to herself.

She stretches out on the floor, opens the Diane Arbus book that Serge lent her. Wait till he finds out she went to his exhibit. Wait till he hears what she has to say about it. She flips to the Halloween picture. A girl with a trick-or-treat bag coming out of a run-down tenement. "The irony is the trick-or-treat bag," she told him. The group had been photographing the homeless in Riis Park. He didn't disagree, except to say that some people would never see it that way because of who they were. She likes it when he turns his furtive black eyes on her.

She dials his number. When he picks up, she says. "It's me, Sara-Jo. And I'm not calling about photography."

▪ The ferry pulls away from the Bayshore dock. The water so choppy she grabs onto the handrail to steady herself. Serge is leaning there, his camera pointed at the receding shore. The wind blows her hair. She hikes up the collar of her jacket, wishing she had a hood. Her ears are freezing.

"Sara-Jo?"

She nods.

"If we go upstairs, we'll get a wider view."

"I'm too cold."

"See the white roll of the waves, like fingers on a piano? I want to capture that." She sees not fingers but a row of little frothing mouths.

"Why don't you wear gloves?"

His hand, chapped red, clasps the camera. "I need the feel of my instrument."

"Like a violin?" Or your penis, she thinks.

"Exactly."

As he turns to go, she slips her arm in his, hides her cold face in the puffy-down sleeve of his jacket.

"Look," he says with evident pleasure, "we're the only ones up here."

"Smart, aren't they? Why are we doing this?"

"The beautiful thing about water is it's like a Rorschach test. Different from every angle."

"If you put your arm around me, you won't be arrested."

"If you're cold, wait for me inside. We'll be on Fire Island in a few minutes." He never looks at her. Never stops clicking the camera.

"Then we can build a fire, rub grease on our bodies, and drape ourselves in sealskins."

"And take pictures of the beach in winter."

His hair's dark, shiny, without even a sprinkle of gray.

"And you'll win a prize for endurance." He glances her way and smiles.

And a joint, she hopes, or at least some red wine.

"Okay, I'm satisfied. Let's go."

She follows him into the pale-green cabin where they wait, leaning on the open door. Outside, just beyond them, the water thrashes.

"Why did you invite me today?"

"To distract you from worrying about your mother's arrival."

"I accept."

"You accept what?"

"That you'll continue to distract, but it's comfort I want."

"I don't blame you."

"Anyway, I'm not distracted, just cold. Can we find some-place to warm up as soon as we get off this tug?" The wind funnels through the doorway, wrapping itself around her face with a wet, stinging force. "The elements are making strong demands," she says, admiring and disliking his lack of discomfort.

Suddenly, the motor's cut. They bob toward an old pier piled with crates and cardboard boxes. Two men stand there, shoulders hunched, hands shoved in pockets, probably wait-

ing to help unload the ferry. She follows Serge to a gate that
swings open when the boat is secured, and hops across onto
the gray-painted boards.

"The beach is about two city blocks from here."

"I'll never make it."

"You will."

They hurry down the narrow path between small boarded-
up bungalows. The wind is fierce. She shields her mouth with
a gloved hand. Ahead the dunes rise into view. She runs down
the rickety steps onto the beach. The black water roars up
through the wind, then disappears into white foam.

He comes up behind her. She leans against him. "When I
was a child, I used to lean like this on my mother. She'd never
let me fall."

"That's what moms are for." He eases her forward, then
kneels, pointing the camera toward the waves.

The tide's high, the sand soft. She circles him, a cat around
a bird. "Take a picture of me."

"Here, hold the camera." He stands behind her, his jacket
open, tenting her against the sandy wind. Her eye pressed to
the lens, she scans the distance, the sky bruised black and
blue, the water churning angrily. She snaps the shutter once.
"I'm coming home with you."

"No reason for that."

She hugs herself, hears *click, click.* What a way to spend a
day together. Photographing. Just photographing. They could
have found something so much nearer and pleasanter, the
park, a bookstore, a movie. What's his story, anyway?

They slog back to the steps. She takes them two at a time.
"You're acting like a priest."

He chortles.

"I don't care to amuse you."

"But you do."

"I want to go home with you."

"Unwise."

"So what? I'm seventeen, not a baby, not a virgin. You must be curious about me. I know you're attracted to me. Your problem is that you grew up when women didn't talk the way I do."

"You don't know my problem."

"You think I can't wait to share everything with my girl-friends. Wrong, Serge. Really wrong. Forget it. I'm fun and good to be with and if you can't see past all the petty dangers to good-time hours with me, I don't want to bother with you either. Let's get off this freezing island. The smart people left here months ago."

She begins walking, looking for the pier. He catches up to her, turns her around, points the other way.

She shrugs his damn hand off her shoulder.

▪ Serge brakes the car in front of a large, wooden house wrapped in a sagging porch, the last one on a street of newer brick homes.

"Here it is. All mine." He turns off the ignition.

"Big place for one person. Must've cost you a lot."

"This is the boonies, my dear. Besides, I rent it."

On the porch, she notices the lack of clutter, not even a chair. "Don't you ever sit out here?"

"That would be too neighborly." He unlocks the front door and leads her down a long, dark hallway. He doesn't turn on a light until they reach the living room at its end. She unzips her jacket, shrugs it off and sprawls on a nubby green couch.

"Sit down, stay a while," she says. "How long have you lived here?"

"A few years."

"And before?"

"Ohio."

"Jail?"

"What?"

"Just kidding. But you're not big on details, are you?"

"I worked for a newspaper."

"Why leave?"

"Bored."

She stares at him. "Divorced, right?"

"Never married."

"Break up a long relationship?"

"None of your business, is it?"

"Ask me about me."

"You're not old enough to have much to tell."

"And your life is so fun?"

"Longer, anyway."

"Serge, sit down, so we can talk."

"In a minute." He walks out.

She eyes a wing-back chair, a piano, the plain white shades rolled all the way up on the bay windows. Does he really live here? Does anyone? His brother? His girlfriend? She rifles through a pile of magazines by the couch. *Details, Double-take, Aperture, Detour.* Maybe the other rooms will tell her something. She wanders warily into the hallway, flips on the light. The walls are lined with posters. Ads for exhibits. She examines the names on them. Rauschenberg. Motherwell. Nothing. They don't seem to be photographers. She opens the closet door. A coat, a shovel, a camera, a pair of cowboy boots.

"Scoping me out?" He places mugs of coffee on the low glass table between couch and chair.

"Did you attend all those shows?" She waves in the direction of the hall.

"You can buy them at any corner museum."

"Did you?"

"No."

"What about the rest of the house?"

"Have a tour."

He doesn't follow her. Older men must respond to different signals, or maybe they know how to keep cool until a woman's totally ready. Guys her age get hard so quickly. It's insulting. That won't happen with him. It'll be a challenge to make him lose control.

She switches on a floor lamp in the bedroom. His jacket is a dark puddle in the middle of the bed. There's another camera on the side table. Maybe there's one in each room, taking pictures all the time like in banks. Her eyes search the room and come to rest on a squat white dresser with three drawers. Does she really want to look at his underpants? If they're folded neatly, she won't like it. If they're balled up or dirty, it'll turn her off. Better not to know. But already her fingers are pulling the top drawer out a few inches. She peeks inside, listening for his footsteps. A layer of folded wool scarves, a dark green one on top. For Serge who doesn't even care about the weather? She slips her fingers in, climbing down the scarves until underneath she feels the soft leather of gloves. Maybe they're all gifts he's stashed away? But from whom? Gently, she nudges the drawer closed. Again she listens for footsteps. Certainly, if she remains in here any longer, he'll come join her.

When he doesn't, she returns to the living room.

"Any surprises?"

She shrugs. "A man living alone. Not even a cat."

"Drink up, then I'll drive you home."

"Also many cameras, many arty posters but no pictures of vets anywhere. How come?"

He looks at her quizzically, his head slightly cocked.

"I went to your exhibit."

His eyes seem more amused than pleased.

"Are they too bleak for home consumption?" she asks.

"I take it you weren't impressed, then."

"That's putting it mildly." She reaches for the coffee mug.

"Tell me more."

"I don't aim to amuse, Serge. My opinions are worth something. In this case particularly."

"Why?"

"The subject is my specialty. Do you have any red wine, or even white?"

He shakes his head. "I'm waiting."

"With bated breath, I hope."

"To the point, my dear. I'm about to lose interest."

She doesn't believe him, not the way he's leaning toward her. "Your shots of the vets aren't grounded."

He says nothing, but she can feel his interest peaking.

"I know what they're capable of, but you show them on permanent vacation. You miss their essence."

"Which is . . . ?" He's staring at her now.

"They lived their whole lives in a year or two. Nothing and no one that came after matters. Not in the same way. Your pictures ignore, maybe even celebrate the ruts they're in. Depressing."

"If you were the photographer?"

"I'd show their children climbing out of their wastelands. That would be life-enhancing."

"Art, Sara-Jo, is more revealing than life. You didn't like what you saw, so you're trashing the photos. I also gather the subject strikes close to home. Might you not be a bit subjective?"

"Yeah, yeah. I'm permanently upset on the topic, and for me to calm down will be forever. But why do you care about *them*?"

"I respect their plight."

"*Their* plight?" Oh Jesus, she prays, don't let him have a brother missing in action. She slides off the couch onto the glass table, wanting to be closer to him, wanting him to touch her. "What about the rest of us?"

"I thought we were discussing photographs?" His eyes seem to harden. Perhaps it's her imagination. He's a little perturbed is all. Well, good. She'll get to him one way or another.

"In none of your pictures is there a child, a wife, a sister, no one but them, only them. Selfishly alone." She flashes on the New Year's Eve photo on Ida's wall. The women with their wide smiles, big eyes, arms never at their sides but always touching each other, touching the men. Even there, the children are missing. "Someday, I'll show you my family album."

"Where's your father now?"

"Park bench. Subway station." She shrugs. "He's probably somewhere on the Lower East Side. There's a bunch of homeless vets there, crazy, homeless vets."

"Pretty hard on him."

"Not hard enough."

"Instead of family photos, maybe you'll introduce me to the real McCoy."

"Why would you want that?"

"Pictures."

"Oh Jesus, Serge, not of him. What's your thing with vets, anyway. Do you have someone . . . ?"

"I had a house once next door to a VA rehab center."

"That's a lame excuse. You listened to their war stories in the local bar and fell in love with them?" She grins.

"You could say that."

"Maybe someday we'll trade war stories."

"I don't have any."

"Then how about sad stories?"

"None of those, either."

"Oh come on, everyone has them."

"Do they?"

"I'll just stay here a little while longer and find out."

"No reason for that."

"I don't believe you."

"You ought to." His voice low.

"Are you worried about me?"

"You aim to get what you want."

"No matter what."

"You might not know what to do with it."

"That sounds sinister. Should I be afraid?"

"It might be a reasonable response," he says, reaching for her jacket.

▪ The plane cuts through the darkness between two highways of shimmering white lights, tearing the cobweb of attachment to California, releasing her into New York. In the cabin, the overhead lights dim. The plane bounces down with a dull thud, the engines roar, then diminish. It taxis toward the terminal, yellow flares as festive as candles leading the way. Snow, hard and graying, is banked along the outer edges of the runway.

Somewhere out there is Sara-Jo. And it scares her. She moves slowly through the accordion-pleated sleeve into the terminal, then follows the signs to the baggage area. Her sister and Ida have smoothed the path ahead, have arranged everything, doctors, tests, the hospital stay. Only the terror remains.

She spots her daughter, waves, glad to see her hair once again close to its natural red and only two rings in each ear.

She takes this as a compliment to her arrival and wraps her arms around the slim shoulders, then steps back. "Looking good, sweetie. Real good." She takes Sara-Jo's hand in both of hers. The blue eyes so like Rooster's, who's out there heaven knows where.

Sara-Jo pulls her hand away, hikes her backpack over a shoulder. "Ida's picking us up in half an hour, straight off her shift. Let's go have a drink."

She follows Sara-Jo into the lounge. A table near the window overlooking the runways. The control tower, with its circling lights, rises out of the darkness.

"The facts, Millie. What's happening to you?"

"They found a tumor, somewhere near the ovary, could be the top of the uterus. It's not clear."

"What else?"

"I'll need surgery."

"Did you get a second opinion?"

"It's there."

"No more children?"

"Sara-Jo!" She can't help laughing. "That's not exactly an issue."

"Will you be real sick?"

"For a while."

"But once they get it out, you'll be fine, right?"

"I might need chemo." She's surprised by the weakness she hears in her whisper.

"And then you'll be fine, right?"

"I could lose my hair."

"It'll grow back.

"Never this long."

"Why not?"

"Never this red again."

"You can't say."

"It'll be gray. The roots already have white in them."

"You can dye it. You're a goddamn beautician."

"We don't need to talk about this now," she mumbles, pushing back the foreboding.

"Mom, we do. Why didn't you have the surgery in California?"

"Everyone's here."

"That's not going to shrink your tumor. I could've flown out. This isn't a great place for you."

"It's home, Sara-Jo."

"A bunch of crazy vets?"

Rooster's eyes stare at her. "Enough."

"The booze, the stupid jokes, the noise of their existence?"

"Stop it."

"You should've moved in with Pete."

"You've never even met him."

"Where's the mystery?"

"At your age it all seems simple."

"It has nothing to do with age. Just choices."

"And you don't like mine?"

Sara-Jo shrugs. "You came home because it feels safer."

"What if it does? God, why are we arguing? I've only known Pete a few months. Do you really expect me to rely on him the same way I do on my family?"

"You might try."

Two children who don't understand, one on each coast, she thinks, and says, "Why is that so important to you?"

"I don't know. Why are you getting so mad?"

"Because your timing is worse than a broken watch."

"I didn't *plan* this conversation."

"What is it that's eating you?"

"Nothing."

She stares hard at her daughter, her jaw clenched against the tears.

"You always think you know more than me."

"Sometimes I do, Sara-Jo."

"Everything gets filtered through *your* experiences. You can't hear me."

So familiar. So expectable. If only she could wrap her arms around her daughter the way she did years ago. But that's not allowed, not anymore, and she hasn't found the words to take its place. In the distance, the planes line up and fly off soundlessly.

"How about I get us something to drink?"

"Mind if I have wine?"

"Yes."

For the first time, Sara-Jo smiles. "I knew that. Coke, then."

At the bar waiting for the drinks she can observe her daughter more carefully. If only she could warn her: We may not have much of a future, please, please, let's make the present sweet. Shit. Perhaps their being apart was only preparation. Thoughts she can't stop are piling up inside her head, heavy as a migraine.

She sets the drinks on the table and looks out the window, to compose herself, to chase away the descending depression.

"Mom, say something."

"I'm tired."

"Say something anyway."

"I was remembering when you were born."

Sara-Jo shifts uncomfortably.

"Maybe because I'm going into the hospital again. I was just remembering how your father bought a case of champagne— I don't know where he got the money—and stood at the nursery offering drinks to anyone who passed by."

"He would."

"He was so happy when you were born."

"Happy? Him?"

"Has anyone seen him?"

"I think Ida has some idea where he is. She wanted to tell him about you."

"Really?"

"She's a hopeless romantic. I wouldn't let her."

"You're too bitter, Sara-Jo."

"You want me to lie?"

"I wish you'd care more, it's healthier."

"If you're concerned about my health, keep him out of this. I don't want him near you."

"Since when are you my boss?"

"Mom. The man's no good. He never was. Why do you think you went so far away?"

She laughs softly, but there's no amusement in it. "To stay warm. To change my life. I can't tell you completely. But believe me it wasn't to leave Rooster. He left me years ago. There was no need for me to cross a continent to do it again." She swallows a mouthful of the wine, which is too warm and a bit sour.

"I met a man, Mom. He runs a photography workshop. He has his own photo exhibit downtown right now. We're seeing each other. Sort of."

"A teacher?"

"Don't reduce him to a label."

"Well, pardon me." She tries to smile.

"He takes pictures of vets, homeless and otherwise. Weird, but it's his calling, I suppose. Anyway, he lives in a big house in Bayshore."

"Really. How old is he?"

"Old enough to be smart."

"I love it when your face lights up that way."

"Don't study me, for God's sake."

"Right. Well, tell me more. Like his name." Her tone as unconcerned as she can make it.

"Serge."

"How nice."

"Mom. It's just a name."

What she says, what she does, matters so much to Sara-Jo. She didn't see that so clearly before. She had no reason to, but now time is precious. She reaches over to press her daughter's hand, decides instead to pluck a napkin from the dispenser.

"I take it Ida's met Serge."

"Why should she? She's not my mother."

Of course not, she thinks, the mother who had the audacity to make a new life for herself. That's not allowed, not until the child has children of her own. "Are you upset being here without me?"

"Not at all. It's good for me."

"And you don't even miss me?" She tries to make it sound like a joke.

"I don't spend time on it, Mom."

Careful, Millie, she warns herself, feeling weepy again. Those eyes staring at her, that hair, the color of her own. Her daughter, a repository of God knows what, of everything. She looks away.

"What's wrong?"

She shrugs.

"Mom, why are you being this way? It's creepy. You're scaring me."

She finishes the wine. "Tell me about Serge."

"There's nothing more to say. It's not like I spend all my time with him. I have college applications to fill out, you know."

"Is anyone helping you?"

"I can do them myself."

Right, she doesn't need input anymore. "Where are you thinking of going?"

"Out of town."

She composes her face into a pleased expression.

"I'll leave in June, get a job wherever. I don't want to hang around Ida's any longer than I have to. And you shouldn't either."

She nods. This is what she wants for Sara-Jo. To make something of herself. It's what Sara-Jo wants, too. They're in total agreement. Except she feels no relief.

"I gather that where exactly you go is less important to you than the going?" Her voice remains an embarrassing whisper.

"I'm investigating the possibilities."

"I see."

"Don't sound like that."

"Like what?"

"Like you're afraid for my future." Sara-Jo never stops watching her.

"Of course I'm not." Or if so, only because her own future feels so threatened. "I'm interested, that's all." She returns her daughter's gaze and decides to say nothing more.

Sara-Jo sits back, crosses her shapely legs clad in black leggings that disappear into short, shiny, yellow boots.

After five more planes take off, Ida will come and save them both. She begins to count.

▪ There'll be no surprises, Sara-Jo promises herself, entering the front door. Sick people look lousy until they get better. She's prepared for all that as well as any tubes or wires that enter or emerge from her mother's body. She knows the hospital. She's had dinner in the employee cafeteria with Ida many times. Ida's given her a pass.

The lobby's bright. The black tile floor slippery under her

boots. She takes the elevator to the fifth floor, room 512, hesitates a moment at the half-open door, then steps in. The DANGER: NO SMOKING sign propped on the window first catches her eyes, then the oxygen capsule like a rocket near the bed. The warm piney-formaldehyde smell nearly gags her.

Except for one arm, her mother's body is hidden beneath a dark gray blanket, only her chin jutting out, small, pointed, and very white. A pale green shower cap stuffed with her mother's long hair puffs out against the pillow. Ribbons of blue vein run up her neck.

Sara-Jo touches the blanket. Her mother's stillness unnerves her. She walks to the closet. Hanging inside is a pantsuit. She fingers the green material, slides her hand into the pockets, pulling out a pair of sunglasses. She roots around in a small canvas bag on the closet floor. Makeup, a comb, brush, toothpaste. She pulls out a small mirror and holds it under her mother's nose, examining the fine mist. Her thumb brushes the back of Millie's hand under the sheet. IV lines snake down from bags of liquid to the other hand, which is taped to a board.

She hurries out to the nurses' station.

"Yes?"

"Room 512. I think her IV's stopped dripping."

"The bag's empty?"

"No. But I can't see any liquid moving."

"Really?"

She follows the nurse into the room, watches her check the IV, then her mother's hand.

"No, dear, it's going down slowly."

"Is the doctor around?"

"The surgeon left. Her doctor will be in to talk to her in the morning."

"Do you know what he's going to say?"

"You'll have to ask him yourself."

"Will she be asleep for long?"

"It's hard to say." The nurse grasps her mother's toes beneath the blanket, gives the leg a sharp shake. No response. "Well, let her be." And closes the door softly.

Sara-Jo goes to the window and looks down at the street, registering nothing. Any fool would have known that the IV was okay. But she's never seen her mother so still. She remembers tiptoeing into the bedroom when she was little to watch her toss and turn. If the door was shut, Rooster was there. Once she went in anyway. His eyes were open. He didn't say a word. She still can't figure out if he knew she was there.

She wants someone to tell her how sick her mother really is. And for how long. She needs her afternoons free to take pictures with Serge. If her mother stays in New York, she'll have to hear he's too old. What kind of man would go out with a girl her age? A real boyfriend would be at her side right now. But Serge isn't a boy, he's a man who expects her to be a woman. And she is. A woman capable of facing a hospital bed by herself.

Pulling up a chair, she stares at her mother's sunken face. People die from cancer. On TV, it takes an hour. Life's different and Millie's strong. She's like her mother that way. But only that way. Millie's tastes are not hers, particularly in men. Still, she mustn't think bad thoughts. Because if she freaks, it won't be good for either of them. She does wish, though, that someone would tell her flat out: Three weeks and Millie will be her old self again. Or whatever. She could page Ida, but Ida will want to know everything inside her head. Trying to figure that out will make her feel like she's drowning in a fish tank. Already the need for air is getting to her.

She presses her mother's arm lightly. She could shake

her, really shake her awake, or call her name until she responds. "Mom. Mom. Mom." Her lips move without sound. Jesus, she'd better get out before she totally spooks herself. Besides, the mob will arrive soon, their false cheer sure to drive her daffy. Let just one tipsy vet put his arm around her like she was still a child and she'll bare her breasts.

Slinging the pack over her shoulder, she leaves the door half-open behind her.

▪ Outside, the wind going right through her, she pulls gloves over icy fingers and hurries down the subway steps. In the token booth, the woman's counting money. No one else around. She sneaks under the turnstile, strides to the far end of the platform.

At Astor Place, she exits the train, the station dusty from renovation, and climbs to the street. Coming here could be a gross mistake. But it's no use warning herself, she's already on her way, following Second Avenue toward Tompkins Square Park, wishing she had a spray can so she could add her words to the lemon-and-lime graffiti along the walls. "Temporary Visitor." "Wide Flyer." "Up and Out." The cluttered, run-down buildings give her the creeps. Not even alleys to separate them. No one could make her live down here.

Across the street in the park she can see the men huddled around flames that flare from a large black barrel. Serge would already be snapping pictures. *Click. Click.*

Rooting around in her backpack, she finds the end of an old joint, lights it, leans against a brick wall, the cold immediately reaching through her jacket. She exhales, her eyes slit into lenses. Yes, Serge's pictures come to life. The men move eerily behind a veil of smoke. But is one of them her father? She takes another drag. Holds it, focusing on the long, dark figure wrapped in a coat that reaches the ground. Through a haze of smoke and cold, she can just make out his familiar beard, longer now, more like a bib across his chest, his hair matted to the shoulders. Who'd want this picture anyway? Not her. She peers harder. What does Serge see in them? He can't know them the way she does. He's an outsider looking in.

Even if it is him, even if he sees her, he won't recognize her. Not after two years. Not after these two years. But it doesn't matter. This is no how-are-you, I'm-fine visit, and the sooner it begins the quicker it will end. She tries to inhale again, but without a clip it's too hot for her frozen fingers. She lets it drop. Smashes it into the pavement with her boot. Then, shoving her hands into her jacket pockets, she crosses the street, kicking angrily at an empty pint bottle by the curb. He's undoubtedly sloshed anyhow.

"Rooster, go ahead, say it for us anyway."

"One foot in the grave, the other still testing the waters. Well, look-y, look-y, someone I know." He peers at her. "Sara-Jo, meet my friends. Arrow, Handy, Marco the White-Haired. He wasn't in our war. And this here's Rush. And the Mayor, his name's actually Sentimental Journey." From somewhere, she hears low laughter. "And this is my main man, Joey. Joey, can you believe him, the bastard was a marine. He thinks he's still walking point for us old grunts. Right?"

Joey waves at her. He's younger than the others. Too young. Rooster can't be telling the truth. The whiskey's probably wiped out what's left of his brain. She eyes the six men. Smoke clouding their mouths, fire reddening their faces. Black ash swirling in the wind. The white-haired man reveals a toothless grin. And she begins walking. This is somebody else's photo.

Rooster catches up to her. "Looking for anyone I know?"

"You."

"How'd you know where?"

"Ida told me Grand Central or this park. I tried here first."

Rooster rumbles out some laughter. "Woman's clairvoyant. Then again, my life's an open book. I just stopped writing in it, that's all."

She keeps distance between them, but her eyes take in his hunched-over body, the fingers long, blackened, hanging from the ragged sleeve of his coat, the dark shoes laced with cord, scuffed into grayness and too big for his feet. The wet hem of his coat is crusted with dirt. He's only a few years older than Serge, but what could he tell her about middle-aged men and sex? Nothing she'd want to hear, she knows that.

"Where to?" he asks, stepping closer.

"Someplace warm." She edges away, afraid to smell him.

He leads her into a harshly lit storefront. They slide into the only booth. On a stool behind a counter is a man so huge there seems to be no room for him to move. His head rests against the wall, his moon face expressionless. She draws her jacket tighter.

Rooster's face is so gaunt, weather-beaten. There's a sore on his cheek, his skin is blotchy, his forehead creased, his eyes stare out of deep hollows. "You look terrible," she tells him.

"Can't say the same for you."

"I'll have tea."

She watches as he leans over the counter, lifts out two tea bags and plastic cups, fills them with hot water from a spigot. He sets one in front of her. She can't tell how juiced he is. "Is that what you do all day? Drink and talk about the war?"

His eyes, two feverish blue lights, fasten on her. "Well, we're men of differing opinions. Arrow says they tied our hands. He likes winning. Can't blame him. Exotic feeling, like papaya and guava. Last time I ate some was, let's see, can't remember. The Mayor, now he's a broken record about all that blood without a killing. Me, I just listen. Do you have a cigarette?"

"Smoking's bad for your health."

"So's living." He doesn't smile.

"Why don't you go into some VA home? Being on the streets is disgusting."

"I've chosen a better way. A witness wandering the world."

"The world? You mean the parks, the subways? Don't make me laugh."

"Levity is not to be sneered at." He drinks the steaming tea straight down. Whiskey's probably killed his taste buds, too. "Girl, you can't just sit here and stare at me. Your mother brought you up better than that."

"Yeah, she did. All by herself." And Millie floats between them, the way she always has, keeping them apart. For better or worse, Sara-Jo will never know.

"You have some message laying hard on your heart?" He leans across the table until his face is inches from hers. "Deliver it." She could easily poke him in the eye, smack his forehead, run her nails down his cheek. Whatever did Millie see here? Where's the spark they all talk about, the one that can illuminate the promise in him? She can't find it. She never could.

He sits back in the booth. "Why'd you come looking for me? Somebody die? Leave me a million? If so, cash the check and keep half. How's that for a tip?" His gravelly laugh shades over into a hacking cough.

"Millie's in the hospital."

"Why?"

"Cancer."

"Murder."

"Don't you want to know where she is?"

"She sees me, she sees trouble."

"You have to be sober."

"Not that hard."

"You can't go looking like this, either."

He stares at her.

"I mean it. Find some place to clean up."

"Shit. Poor bird. Name the hospital, Sara-Jo. No more, no less."

"New York Hospital. Be there. Sixty-eighth Street and York Avenue. Millie doesn't know I came here. I couldn't tell her. She wouldn't wake up, didn't even move a finger. She could have been dead."

He turns his eyes on her. "Where you staying?"

"You can't come there."

"Don't tell me what I can or can't do, girl."

"Oh Jesus, this isn't about me and you. Don't you want to see her?"

"Answer's too long for this lifetime."

"Tell me anyhow, I have a right to know."

"Suppose you do. Suppose you do? What of it?" He turns to gaze out the dirt-streaked window. "Pretty Millie." He shakes his head. "Poor bird."

Suddenly, the heat seems to thicken around her and she doesn't want to talk to him anymore, doesn't even care if he sees Millie or not. It's their lives, their business, and the only thing she needs to do is get far away from here. Quickly. She slides out of the booth. "I have to go."

"Say good-bye, Sara-Jo."

But she's already out the door, walking fast toward the station.

When the train pulls into Bayshore, she's at the door, trying to pry it open. She runs down the escalator steps to the phone, dials Serge's number, the receiver pressed to her ear.

He says hello twice before she answers. "It's me. I'm at the station, taking a cab to your place."

"Wait a minute."

"I've just seen my father. I've been all over. How much will it cost, the cab?"

"About six dollars."

"I don't have it."

"I'll wait outside."

He's there, not wearing a jacket. He pays the driver. She scoots ahead, lest he change his mind and send her home. In the living room her eyes slide to the same neat pile of magazines on the floor, this time topped by a paperweight of green stone that looks for all the world like kryptonite, but maybe it's jade or glass. As always, the table tops are clear, no junk, no dust, no mess anywhere. Clean is good right now.

He stands in the doorway, his bare feet stuffed into sweet suede moccasins.

"Aren't you cold?" she asks.

"Why should I be?"

Yeah, he's right. They're indoors, aren't they? She'd better calm down. She's perturbed, disgusted, revolted, but not with him, not at all with him. "Thanks for having me."

"Coffee?"

She shakes her head. Dope, she thinks, but he might not appreciate it.

"How's your mother?"

"She didn't look good."

"People don't after surgery."

She could ask how he knows, but doesn't want to hear hospital stories.

"Yeah. Well, I left her asleep." She pats the couch, but he sits in the chair.

"I didn't expect you," he admits.

"So, anyway, if you're still my friend . . ."

"Yes?"

"I'd like a drink."

"There's beer in the fridge."

She takes off her boots, walks slowly past him into the kitchen. No dirty dishes. No leftover food. Nothing extra. She takes out a can of beer. Tsing Tao. She's never heard of it. Probably expensive, too. Where does he shop, anyway? She lifts the tab and takes a swallow. Pretty smooth-tasting. She opens the freezer and peers in. Leaning on an ice tray is a white envelope. With her thumb she gently flips up the flap and sees a wad of money, tens, twenties, fifties. Where did he get all this? Surely not from giving workshops. Two more swallows of beer and she returns to the couch.

"There's money in your freezer."

"A safe place."

"How'd you get it?"

"I lead a pack of thieves."

"Seriously."

"Odd jobs."

"Odd photos? Like porn?"

He stares at her and then laughs. "It's none of your business."

"Of course it is."

"Sara-Jo, adults know better than to ask about people's money."

"Are you insinuating something about my youth?"

"Indeed."

"Come on, tell me, where'd you get all that cash?"

"Trust fund." His eyes hold hers, intense, challenging.

"You're kidding?" It's not the way she imagines a rich man living. She looks again at the furniture. Is there something she's missed? Even Ida's living room is grander.

"How did that happen?"

"My grandparents."

"What did they do?"

"Enough, Sara-Jo."

"So you can take off, anywhere, anytime? Someday I'm going to have money, too. And I'm going to use it to do whatever I want." She sits on the arm of his chair.

"It's not good for you to hang out here."

"Okay. I'm warned." She leans over, plants a light kiss on his mouth, then returns to the couch. Maybe he'll follow, sit beside her. With Carlos she could predict every move—except the army, of course. "Either you want to be with me or you don't," she tells him.

"Those aren't the only choices."

"That's the way I see it, unless you're still playing Mr. Priest."

"You don't understand the first thing about me." He smiles that damn smug smile and walks out.

"What's to know," she mutters, then sees the CD player and begins browsing through some disks. Operas. She should've brought her Walkman. She listens for his footsteps. What can he be doing? And why would a man keep his trust fund in the freezer? Rich man, poor man, beggar man, thief. None of it makes any sense. Maybe he wants her to follow him. She has no idea. He could be shy, but she doubts it, or maybe he needs time to prepare himself, except she doesn't believe that either. Maybe he just needs to be certain that she's really willing, otherwise he's committing whatever with a minor. After all, she could report him. But only for not loving her, for mysteriously avoiding a very ready young woman who wants to give and take pleasure.

So where the hell is this Mr. Noble saving her from a lecherous affair? She doesn't want to be saved, just transported out of the misery of her day. For all she knows, he's fled through the back door.

"Serge!" she calls far too loudly as she enters the kitchen. For he's there looking out the window. She slides her arms around his waist. "Don't worry. It'll be okay. I'm not a child. You must know that." His lean body excites her.

Suddenly the small pot on the stove begins to shake. He picks it up and pours coffee into a mug, then takes a bottle of vodka from the cabinet, and pours that in, too. Looking at his face, she can't tell if he's excited or in pain. And again wonders if all older men are this restrained. Because except for her father, who's a barometer of zilch, the vets never seemed like this and they're just a few years older than him. A flicker of doubt crosses her mind, but that's silly, here she is, isn't she? He didn't invite her, but he sure as hell let her in, even paid for her cab.

From the living room doorway she watches him slug down his molotov cocktail. "You always douse your coffee?"

"You bet," he says, but won't look at her. She's beginning to feel unwanted here. The disappointment hurts. If she goes home without a night to remember, without the pleasure of his arms, tomorrow and the day after will be long and boring. And lonely. And if there's a disaster with Millie? She'll need his loving. She sits cross-legged on the floor in front of his chair. "Can I have a sip?"

He hands her the cup.

She takes a very long, bitter gulp.

"Hey." He pulls it back.

She smiles. "I always take the most I can get before it's gone. It's a habit."

"I have habits, too. I'm not like the boys you hang out with."

"You're older."

"Not just that."

"Then what?"

He gazes past her.

"Listen," she says. "I don't want to think. About Millie. About cancer. About death. About my father. About you. I want to be beyond thought. I want to be one of those piano fingers of yours on the sea."

"What *are* you talking about?"

"You don't remember your own images, but I do. I remember every photo you've taken with me. I took photos all day today. In my head, and there wasn't a piano finger among them and none of the images I saw resembled yours at all. Mine were broken and dirty and who wants them and they don't want anyone either, and there's a white-hot spot right behind my eyes and you better damn well do something right now or you won't like the photos I take of you." She rises to her knees, placing her hands on his thighs. "I saw six men around a caldron tonight." She moves as close to him as the chair will allow, her fingers climbing up his thighs.

"Daring, aren't you?"

"Yeah, well, that's not resolvable. Don't you want to hold me?"

"First, another drink."

Shit, she thinks, he's going to be drunk in a few minutes. That's no fun. She follows him into the kitchen, although it's against her style. She doesn't like running after anyone, man or woman. Besides, he's supposed to want her, too. If he doesn't get with it soon, she'll have to take off. Self-respect and all that. If only Millie were well, she could ask her how older men turn on. Her mother wouldn't like the question, but she'd answer it like she always does. It would be such a relief if someone could tell her everything's going to be all right. Then she wouldn't have to think at all. Her mother could just be there, the way she's supposed to be.

His cup is already half-empty. She needs to move fast. His pale green shirt is buttoned to the neck, she undoes two buttons, slides her hand inside, feeling the bare skin of his chest. "How about another swallow of your drink," she says, "a short one."

"Sleeping with a minor is bad, getting her drunk is stupid."

"Well, then." She can't stop the grin spreading across her face. "I'm about to take a shower. You can dry me," she calls back.

But he's not there when she steps out of the bathroom. And wrapped in the towel she goes into the bedroom. He's under a sheet, the bedspread and blanket in a heap on the floor, his pants folded neatly over a chair, his shirt on a hanger outside the closet, his moccasins, where are they? The blinds are pulled tight but the floor lamp in the corner casts a sweeping arc of ever-softening light on the ceiling where he's gazing, which gives her the creeps. Carlos would have been all over her before she could take another step. But this is Serge, she reminds herself, and the newness excites her even more. She drops the towel, slides in next to him. Abruptly he turns toward her. "I want you to see me." And rolls back the sheet, his prick swollen, ready. *See* him? Why? He should be caressing *her*. What's wrong with him? As if the answer's out there, she looks quickly around the room.

"Don't be afraid. I won't hurt you, I promise." He pulls her toward him, but she inches back, fear cold in her stomach.

"Jerk you off? Is that it?" She speaks matter-of-factly because she senses that any sign of fear will only make things worse. Dogs are like that, too, they attack frightened people. Rooster taught her that. She has to get out of here.

"No. Not that." His voice low, intense.

"Then what?"

"Under the bed." His eyes are on her. "There's a rope."

"I don't do that stuff."

"You can't leave now." He wraps her wrists in his hands. In the dim light, his face moves close to hers.

"Can we talk awhile?" she asks softly.

"What is there to say?" His breath on her lips, his eyes not seeing, his flat body tight against hers.

"Oh, I don't know. Is this why you never married?"

She won't let him hurt her.

"Too late, Sara-Jo."

"For what?"

"To learn the facts of my life."

She could scream, but who would hear her?

"No more talking. Get the rope." His heavy prick against her belly.

"If I don't?"

"It's not an option." He tightens his grip. "Under the bed."

"Then what?" she whispers.

"Hit me with it."

"And after that?" Her dry mouth thickening each word.

"Finished."

She takes a deep breath. He better not be lying. "Okay, let go." She reaches under the bed and touches the rope coiled like a snake. He turns his back to her, begins jerking off. The whole damn bed is shaking.

"Go on," he says, "go on."

He's working his prick like a piston. She prays he comes fast.

"Sara-Jo," he warns, his voice stern, but far away.

Her eyes slide to the wall, to a large poster where red, black, and silver drip into each other and pool in the middle like blood in a dish.

"Go on, go on, go on," his voice rising.

She swings the rope lightly across his buttocks.

"Harder, harder."

Suddenly, it's what she wants to do, beat him until he bleeds to death. She holds the rope with both hands, like cops hold their guns. There's heat in her body, in her face. She strikes him again and again and again, then gasps because his body is now very still. She's killed him. She flings the rope across the room. "God almighty." She jumps out of bed, frantically gathering her clothes, her eyes glued to his back until he flips over.

"Don't go."

His voice erases her fear. "Why, do you have something special in mind?"

"I'll take some photos. On the bed. It'll turn you on."

"Oh, please."

"I want to."

"I should take some of you, then stick them up your . . . No, better yet, I should stick them up on the wall next to the other perverts you captured with your precious camera."

"Sara-Jo, calm down."

"Why, you going to tie me up? I could have been a man for all you cared. Right?"

"Maybe."

"Great, just great. You could have told me. Shit." She pulls the shirt over her head.

He sits up.

"Do me a favor, okay? Stay in bed until I get out of here."

She finds her boots in the living room. The whole thing had nothing to do with her. She was just a hired hand. Hah. That's a laugh. It could've been worse. He could have smacked her around. Who knows? If there were clues she missed them. Waiting until she was naked in bed to share his problem. Jesus, if the vets ever heard about this, they'd tear up the place. Next man she meets, she's going to ask some very probing questions.

She marches into the kitchen, opens the freezer, and lifts a couple of twenties out of the envelope. "Trust fund, my ass," she mumbles. This'll pay her cab fare home. If there's change, big deal, she'll buy her mother flowers.

▪ The door opens. "Hey, pretty lady." He walks in wearing a plaid flannel shirt and a pair of new-looking brown trousers. His overcoat, balled up under his arm, he deposits on a chair. Even his shoes are shined. Somewhere, just beyond Millie's head, the phone rings.

"Rooster." A croak. His face—smooth, plucked, vulnerable, worn—makes her wonder if she's hallucinating. Yet she hears the normal grating, rolling, clanking sounds from the corridor. Her limbs are heavy, her lips dry. There are red roses in a vase at the foot of her bed. On the windowsill two leafy plants. Out the window it's dark.

The phone's still ringing. He reaches across her, whiskey on his breath, lifts the receiver and presses it into her hand. But whoever it was has hung up.

"Must be a wrong number." He takes the receiver from her and hangs up, watching her with Sara-Jo's eyes.

"Some water." Her tongue thick.

He holds the cup under her chin, a slight tremor in his hands. She sips a few drops through a straw.

"A little more won't dry the reservoir."

She shakes her head, licks her lips. "Your beard?"

"You never did like it."

The cadence of his voice lodged forever in her brain.

"So, baby, how you doing?" He pulls a chair up, so close his knees bang into the mattress. "Can't you sit up or something?"

"Not yet."

"Pain?"

"Some."

"Let's call in the meds, get you some drugs."

"Soon." She's touched that he's come, but wouldn't care now if he left. That's a new feeling, not caring. Perhaps there's no way to cut open a body and expect it to come together again just the way it was.

"These places make me wormy." One leg is bouncing now. Probably too juiced to keep steady.

"Worse than the streets?"

"Hardly hear a thing there for all the noise. Besides, it doesn't matter, the sirens, the engines, it's not my house on fire." He lifts his hand but thank God doesn't touch her. He pats the bed instead.

"A little pale is all," he mumbles, his eyes searching the room. "Why all these weird lines?" He gestures at the IVs. "Man, they're alien. This is one small room for a sick person."

"How did you find out about me?"

"Your girl did the right thing."

"Sara-Jo?" Her daughter searching through the tunnels of the city? A frightening picture, yet so fulfilling she can hardly hold onto its enormity.

"Did you and Sara-Jo talk?"

"Like two poets in an alley."

"I told her about you serving me champagne in the hospital when she was born."

"Bet you didn't tell her how I sneaked into your room and slept on the floor all night. Gave that nurse quite a fright."

"It was your fatigues that did it. She probably thought you had a gun." Don't soften, she warns herself, or he'll park here all day.

"Those were good days."

"We didn't have many."

"Don't be extreme."

"A few."

"I made you laugh."

"And cry."

"I kept your soul on fire."

"You sapped my energy."

"You were my main bird, Millie, the only one."

"I believe that."

"Then we're getting somewhere."

"We don't have anywhere to get, not anymore."

"Hey, now, don't set me to trial and find me guilty. Prison's no place for me. No cages, no trenches, no houses, no walls."

No present, no future, no anything for us, she marvels, because there's actually nothing she needs to tell him.

"My wings burn close to the body, remember?" He lifts his arms, flaps his hands.

"Yes, I remember. No cargo allowed on that plane."

"Free spirit is my name," he finishes the chant, the one he always whispered in her ear before disappearing.

"Is that still your name?"

"I'm working my way there."

With nothing to give up, maybe he'll make dying easy.

He walks around the bed, opens the closet door.

"What are you looking for?"

"A radio, some music to cheer you up, get some color into those cheeks, chase away all these unnatural attachments, make you real again." He places his arms in dancing position, twirls around once, bangs into the table at the foot of the bed, catching the vase before it tips over. "Whoa, losing balance, getting old."

"Doesn't everybody?"

"You sound like your daughter."

"She's yours, too."

"Heh, heh. In a manner of speaking. Sure is one tiny room." He stretches out his arms. "Need to hold these walls apart or they'll crush you." He begins coughing.

She wonders if he'll pass out.

He slides onto the windowsill, eyeing the oxygen tank.

"Little bomb," he says and reaches out hesitantly to touch it. Then he unfolds his coat, pulls a half-pint bottle from the pocket, and takes a swallow. "My medicine. And what can I get for you, my lady? The nurse? The doctor? Some water? You tell me. If it's not within my means, I'll search out the means. Understand?"

She nods.

"I'm doing my visit the only way I can." His eyes ablaze.

"I know."

Suddenly he grabs the back of the chair to steady himself. His face so gaunt, she can almost feel the skeleton beneath.

He lifts his coat and wads it once more under his arm. "You'll be clacking on those high heels again." He touches her forehead. "Where you going to be? Lucy's? Ida's?"

She stares at him. "California" comes out of her mouth. Her eyes slide to his thin, trembly fingers, dirty nails. Whiskey and demons, that's who he is. It has nothing to do with her, not anymore.

"You be good now." He walks out just missing a straight line, leaving the door wide open. Two nurses chatter past her room. They'll be in soon enough wanting her to sit up, perhaps even to walk. The doctor, too, should arrive in the morning with news. Then everyone else will be in to see her, a thousand connections to keep her on this planet.

■ Crossing the two-lane highway, Sara-Jo readies herself to sprint, but there isn't a car in sight. She reaches the shoulder of hard-pressed snow, yellowed and slippery, and begins to pick her way uphill toward the mall. It must be nearly 6:00 A.M. She's not sure, except the pale gray light of dawn is opening around her, and white streaks are beginning to crack the dark blanket of sky. She's been walking west on Sunrise Highway for at least two hours. Several cars did stop to offer her a lift, but she's had enough strangeness for one night. Never mind. She'll waste no more time. Serge is now the past. And the past, like old clothing, can be rolled up and stored.

Squinting, she can just make out the diner, lit up like a lamp in a fog. Behind it, the brick façade of the mall. Hot coffee, first, then blueberry pancakes. She blows a few puffs of warm breath into her cupped hands, then stuffs them back into her jacket pockets, still seeing her blue-and-white gloves on Serge's kitchen table. Damn and too bad. For her frozen fingers and because she didn't want to leave him even a scrap of herself.

As she hits flatter ground, she breaks into a trot, wondering if the diner is really there or only a mirage. She takes its three steps in a single bound and tugs open the door, to be greeted by the welcome smell of bacon. She slides into a back booth. Across the narrow aisle an old woman sits alone, her long, white hair braided and wrapped around a large head. One feathery earring touches her shoulder. The woman leans toward her and whispers, "Give me some money and I'll tell you your fortune. At your age, it's mostly good luck."

"I don't believe in luck. How much?"

"Whatever you can spare is my good luck."

Sara-Jo smiles.

With effort, the woman inches her large bulk out of her booth and into the seat facing Sara-Jo. She holds a pack of cigarettes.

"No smoking in here, right?"

"These are Micky Mouse." The woman shifts closer.

"Excuse me?"

"Not real. Five-and-dime store, make-believe chocolate cigarettes. You live around here?"

"For the time being. Does the owner know you tell fortunes?"

"I don't do it in front of his face. I dishwash three mornings a week for a few bucks, and get to sit here all winter. Make a fist."

Sara-Jo obeys.

The woman weighs it in her hand. "Good heft. You need heft when you're young, also when you're old. It's not important in middle age."

"Why?"

"You're on top of the hill. You need it going up and you need it coming down." The woman taps her fist. "Unclench."

"Do I have a long life-line?"

"I don't believe in life-lines, just journeys. First, you must know where you've been." The woman turns her hand over, massages the knuckles. "You have fighter's bones."

"I do, don't I?" she says more to herself than the woman. "Am I leaving soon?"

"Only the old leave." The woman's dark eyes beneath thick white brows look past her. "The old leave everything, even their breathing."

"I don't understand."

"You're not tired enough to understand." The dark eyes settle on her.

"Are you putting me on?"

Again the woman studies her palms. "Your journey began last night."

"What?" She hears her own quick breathing.

"You manage without being prepared. That's your strength. It always will be." Suddenly the woman sits back, plucks out a cigarette, sticks it between her lips, takes it out again. "If I concentrate, I can imagine a few puffs."

"Why not smoke the real stuff?"

"Too expensive."

Sara-Jo feels around inside her jacket pocket, pulls out a twenty-dollar bill and hands it to her.

"I'll bring you coffee. It costs me nothing."

She watches the woman shuffle toward the counter, then her eyes slide to the window, to the flat, unbroken gray sky, to the naked tree limbs between tall black telephone poles. When she reaches the top of the hill, her view is going to be spectacular. That's for damn sure.

ACKNOWLEDGMENTS

I am very grateful to those people who offered their sensitivity, time, support, and guidance: Tom Engelhardt for his ability to hear the voices in my head and for his brilliant editorial skills; Barbara Schneider, George Blecher, Marsha Taubenhaus, Liz Gewirtzman, Judi Dallas, and Frieda Trestman for their never-ending belief in me; Charles Wiggins, for listening through all my crises and giving me the love to carry on; Georgina, for being the light of my life.

And finally, for their moral, editorial, and emotional support as well as for their enthusiasm, I wish to thank Ann Godoff, my editor, and Melanie Jackson, my agent.

BEVERLY GOLOGORSKY has been an activist in the women's and peace movements. She lives in New York, and works in legal-medical publishing. She spends a good deal of time in New England, where her partner, Charles Wiggins, lives. She has a daughter, Georgina.

ABOUT THE TYPE

This book was set in Fairfield, the first typeface from the hand of the distinguished American artist and engraver Rudolph Ruzicka (1883–1978). Rudolph Ruzicka was born in Bohemia and came to America in 1894. He set up his own shop, devoted to wood engraving and printing, in New York in 1913 after a varied career working as a wood engraver, in photoengraving and banknote printing plants, and as an art director and freelance artist. He designed and illustrated many books, and was the creator of a considerable list of individual prints—wood engravings, line engravings on copper, and aquatints.